Don't Let Me Go

An Otter Bay Novel
Jodi Artzberger

Don't Let Me Go

ISBN 9781736583937 (ebook)
ISBN 9781736583944 (paperback)

www.JodiArtzberger.com

This is a work of fiction. Names, characters, places, and incidents either are
the products of the author's imagination or are used fictitiously. All characters
are fictional, any resemblance to actual persons, living or dead, businesses,
companies, events, or locales is entirely coincidental.

Cover design by Jodi Artzberger.

Edited by Paula Grundy.
Proofread by Terry Grundy.

Scripture quotations taken from the New American Standard Bible®
(NASB), Copyright © 1960, 1962, 1963, 1968, 1971, 1972, 1973, 1975, 1977,
1995 by The Lockman Foundation. Used by permission. www.Lockman.o
rg.

Contents

"So faith comes from hearing, and hearing by the word of Christ."
—Romans 10:17

One

"And we know that God causes all things to work together for good to those who love God, to those who are called according to His purpose." Romans 8:28

Jenny gripped the cross that hung around her neck. White and red topaz stones dug into her hand. If she could touch the heavens above, she'd ask again . . . *Why, God?* It was a prayer she begged to have answered.

She wanted to go back. She wanted back the life she could never have again.

Her wedding set rolled around her finger when she caressed and cradled it. The right to wear it was stripped from her when she'd asked Adam for a divorce, but she couldn't bring herself to take it off.

Empty. Numb. Hollow. She didn't want to feel, yet the tears still found a way to break free. Clamping her eyes shut, like trying to chase away a bad dream, she inhaled through her nose, held it, then exhaled through her mouth, rebuilding the dam.

The bay was empty, and the hustle and bustle in the emergency room had now settled. What was once a clamoring department of patients and hospital workers was now almost peaceful.

A welcomed chill from the cool metal frame of the ambulance bay door propped Jenny up. Fresh air nipped at her lungs, and the last of the day's amber hues faded into the night before her. She leaned her head against the doorframe and let her eyes drift closed, and the tension began to drain away.

When she opened her eyes, red and white flashing lights lit up the dark sky as an ambulance crested the hill. Sirens blared, and an Otter Bay Police Department SUV followed.

Nurse Greene jogged through the ambulance bay doors. "Come with me. They're bringing in a single GSW."

Great, another gunshot victim.

Jenny pushed herself off the doorframe, gave her hands a good shake, and stretched out her fingers, waiting for relief from the pins and needles that had invaded her hands like they had fallen asleep.

"You coming?" Nurse Greene asked.

The ambulance braked to a stop as Jenny snapped on a pair of gloves and met the opening doors when the gurney was being lowered.

A very familiar voice spoke behind her, and her heart pounded as warmth spread through her body. She took those feelings and quickly bottled them up. They didn't belong, and she didn't deserve to have them. There was no future for her and Adam. Forever wasn't real. And as long as she didn't look at him, she could hold it together, or so she told herself. With her head down, she prayed for strength and for the injured person in front of her.

Adam eased up next to her. "He was holding up Johnson's Liquor. The call came in requesting backup. We were in the area."

His jacket brushed Jenny's arm, and her nerves pinged off each other, rippling down her spine. Forcing air into her lungs, she asked, "Who shot him?"

As Jenny tugged the gurney up the ramp leading into the emergency room, she stumbled, then righted herself before she hit the concrete. Adam reached out to help her, but she staggered backward out of his grip. Concern flashed in his baby blues. Her hand shot up to stop him from getting closer.

Jenny would give just about anything to run into his strong, comforting arms. Where had her resolve gone? She was doing the right thing. Adam had to see it. One day, he'd understand.

Adam's eyebrows pinched together. "Johnson, the owner, shot him." Adam hesitated, and his head tilted a tick; concern showed in his eyes. "Hey, when your shift is over, maybe we could grab something to eat?"

"Harry Johnson?" Jenny questioned as she fussed with the sheet covering the man on the gurney.

"Yes." He nodded to the man on the stretcher. "Mr. Wild Turkey, as he calls himself, was slashing a knife around like Zorro. Johnson got nervous."

The wheels of the gurney squeaked as it rolled along the linoleum floor of the emergency room. Jenny steered the gurney into the main area, keeping her eyes on the gunshot victim. "I didn't know he could shoot."

"He can't," Adam deadpanned.

Jenny stopped the gurney next to an empty bed in the ER and inspected the wound. The blood had almost stopped on its own. Mr. Wild Turkey might need a few stitches in his upper arm, but there was clearly no bullet in there. "Was anyone else hurt?"

"No. The guy was strung out and looking for some fast cash." Adam glanced at the man on the gurney. "Right now, I'd say he's coming off of whatever he was on."

Ryker stowed his phone as he approached. "A uniform will be here soon to watch him and bring him down to the station when he's released."

"We never saw anything like this growing up here. Our beautiful little community is being overrun with drugs and destroying lives." Jenny focused her attention on Ryker.

Nurse Greene pulled the curtain back and fastened it to the wall. "Detectives, security will watch him until he can be stitched up. Jenny, will you check on the patient in bed four?"

Jenny pulled off her gloves and tossed them in the trash. "Excuse me, gentlemen," she said as she took off in a sprint to her new patient, willing her feet to move, wanting to put some distance between herself and Adam.

The privacy curtain was pulled closed. She slipped around it and reached for the chart. But it wasn't tucked in the bin at the end of the bed. The bedsheets and blanket weren't rumpled; the chart was missing and so was the patient.

"I must have misheard. Seeing Adam is really messing with me," Jenny exhaled and rubbed her tired eyes.

She took a step back to leave when an arm curled around her throat. "Don't say a word and you live. Got it?" a low, gravelly voice whispered in her ear as he raised his other hand in front of her face, holding a full syringe.

Her eyes latched on to the syringe, and a muscle under her eye twitched.

The man loosened his hold and turned Jenny to face him.

Soulless, calculating hazel eyes stared back at her. A dark beard masked most of his face, and disheveled, thick, brown hair covered his head. Mud encrusted his jeans and work boots, his denim jacket ripped and frayed.

"Now, we are going to walk out of here, and you're not going to say or do a thing that will alert anyone. Understand?"

"O-o-okay," Jenny's lips quivered and her heartbeat crashed in her ears. "What do you want from me?" If she left with him, she knew she was as good as dead. She saw his face.

Was Adam still here? Could she get his attention?

"You'll find out soon enough. Let's go!" He leaned in next to her ear: "And don't do anything you'll regret." His voice carried a low-pitched warning that sent every hair on the back of her neck on end.

The man spun Jenny around, and with his arm cradled around her back, he clutched her by the upper arm. His hand wrapped over the syringe, pressing the tip of the needle against her bicep. "Make sure you smile on the way out."

The curtain rings shrilled on the channel as he pulled them open. A shiver raced down Jenny's spine to her toes.

Neither one of their steps echoed as they headed down the corridor. Jenny looked for Adam or Ryker or the uniformed policeman—even a security guard.

The hall was empty.

"I said smile, sweetheart."

Jenny swallowed and tried to regulate her breathing. How could she get someone's attention? They were heading for the back doors, and if they got outside in the dark, she'd lose her chance.

The man picked up his pace and dragged Jenny out the back doors. Cold air pricked her skin through her thin scrubs, and the breeze stole any remaining warmth that her uniform offered. Her steps faltered as they crossed the small staff parking lot. His grip tightened, and he jerked her across the asphalt. Jenny's feet slowed like she'd stepped into quicksand when they reached the wooded area behind the hospital. Her foot tangled with her abductor's foot when she tried to reverse course. "I-I-I can't go in there!"

The man yanked Jenny back. "Are you trying to get yourself killed? Do you think I won't kill you right here and now?"

"I-I-I—"

"Move!" the man growled.

Jenny forced her feet into motion, careful not to get caught up in the low-lying shrubs and tree roots. "D-do-don't you want to go to my car?"

"I have my own. This way," he said as he towed her through the underbrush.

Low-hanging tree limbs that were barely budding for the coming spring scratched through her scrubs and dug into her skin as they made their way to the other side of the woods. Goose bumps climbed up her arms like ivy, covering every inch of flesh. The man led Jenny down an embankment to a dilapidated, rusted-out, two-door, seventies-style sedan sitting next to the curb.

"Your chariot awaits," he said as he opened the door. "Now, get in."

Jenny knew if she got in, it would be the end for her.

Her eyes darted around, looking for anyone. There was nothing to see but darkness and an empty street.

No one to help her.

She turned to run and ran straight into a wall of solid muscle—blocked between her captor and his car.

Nowhere to run.

"I thought you might try something like that." He pulled out a pair of handcuffs, slapped one cuff on her wrist, and shoved her into the car. He slid the other cuff through the door handle and cuffed her other wrist. "Don't make this any harder than it needs to be." His words crawled over her before he leaned back out of the car and slammed the door shut.

Jenny reached for the door latch lever and met air. It was gone!

She threw her shoulder into the door, then looked behind her. The door lock was gone too.

The driver's side door opened, and he slid into the driver's seat. Without looking her way, he said, "You can stop. It's not going to open. I made sure of that." Holding up the syringe, he said, "And I don't recommend you scream either."

The car whirred to life, and he pulled away from the curb, turning north. "Get comfortable. We've got a little drive ahead of us. It will be awhile before anyone notices you're gone."

The last time Jenny had been on this road was when she'd followed Adam's partner, Ryker, and his wife, Amanda, to his dad's cabin. Amanda had just left the hospital after someone had tried to kill her.

Jenny watched the trees speed by until the overgrown treetops wove themselves together like fingers interlaced in prayer, blocking out the moon and the stars.

Jenny rubbed her hands together, closed her eyes, and bowed her head.

"Are you praying?" The man snickered. "That won't help you. No one'll find you where we're going. And even if they do—March in Maine is still winter. You'll freeze before anyone can rescue you."

A lone tear trickled down her cheek; her strangled, scared-little-girl voice cried, "What do you want? I'll do anything, please. Please don't hurt me."

Has anyone noticed I'm not there? Is anyone looking for me?

Adam filled her thoughts. She wanted to hear his voice and feel his arms wrapped around her.

Please Lord, let someone find me; let Adam be looking for me.

The car turned off the main road and kept going. As it continued to weave around the back roads, Jenny lost track of where they were. The darkness closed in on them—on her. Finally, he came to a stop next to an old service road gate that looked like it had long since been forgotten.

Darkness that blanketed the car was sliced open by its headlights and reflected off a No Trespassing sign that illuminated the interior of the car.

Jenny took her eyes off the road and watched the man. More tears fell. The handcuffs chafed her wrists and rattled against the door handle as she shook.

A slow smile crept into place when he turned and faced her. He settled back into the seat, and with a grand sweeping gesture of his hands, he said, "This is it."

"This is what?" Panic filled every crevice of Jenny's body and strangled her voice.

"The end. It's the end of the road for you." He stretched his arm across the back of the bench seat and leaned over toward her.

She plastered herself next to the door, gripping and wrestling with it. Tears freely flowed down her cheeks, and in between gasps of air, Jenny said, "No, please, no! Please!"

And for the first time, his eyes lit up and danced with amusement.

Jenny's scream began in her toes, and by the time it reached her mouth, sounded like it could split the sky. The more she yanked on the door, the more her body vibrated.

He slid closer and caressed her cheek with the back of his hand. "You really are quite beautiful. But you probably know that, don't you? All the pretty ones do."

She squeezed her eyes shut; pain shot through her chest like someone was sitting on it. Her face drenched with tears. "Please! No! Stop! Whatever you're planning, please don't do it."

"Oh, you have no idea what my plans are," he purred in her ear.

Jenny's heart stopped at his words. She fought to free herself—wildly pulling and straining against the cuffs that jangled with every move.

She had to get away from him.

He picked up the syringe, his smile turned wicked, and he plunged the needle into her thigh through her scrubs.

She froze, eyes on her thigh. One look at her captor, and a whisper escaped, "What did you do?"

"This won't take long now." He caressed her cheek one more time, then slid back behind the steering wheel.

Two

Barbed wire twisted around Adam's heart, and every prick of the wire pierced and squeezed. He leaned against the wall outside the hospital's security office and rubbed at that spot on his chest over his heart.

Where is Jenny?

He shoved off the wall, and his steps thundered through the concrete hallway. He jammed his hands into the front pockets of his jeans and his wedding ring caught. The chair next to the security office clattered on the concrete floor when he dropped into it. The fluorescent light bounced off his platinum band.

Why didn't I wait for her? This is my fault, all of it.

The chair banged into the dingy cinder-block wall when he stood and resumed his pacing. The muscles in his jaw tensed the more he replayed seeing Jenny earlier.

The hall closed in on him as his strides turned into a stomp.

Why didn't someone stop Jenny? Why didn't he wait for her? Why didn't he go after her? Why didn't someone at least ask where she was going or who she was with? All of her belongings, even her cell phone, were all still at the nurses' station.

Where is she?

"Security ready for us?" Ryker asked as he jogged down the stairs.

A low, guttural noise pushed free. "No. How hard is it to pull some footage from a few hours ago?" Adam turned toward the security office, and the door swung open before he could knock.

"Detective Taylor, Detective Scott, come in. I believe we found all the footage," Dak Miller said and stepped back as Adam pushed through the door.

The room shrank with Adam, Ryker, and Miller standing in front of the two monitors. With his arms crossed over his chest, Adam's eyes locked on the two screens in front of him. "This is all you have?" Both monitors showed the cameras that were focused on the back doors that led to the employee parking lot, on pause.

"We're a small operation," Miller said. "You know that. You're not new around here, Detective. We'll find Jenny."

"We'd better! I can't believe no one saw her leave last night." Adam snapped as he stared at the screen, that was frozen in time.

"Easy," Ryker interjected. "You're not going to do Jenny or yourself any good if you lead with your emotions."

Adam took a deep breath and closed his eyes when he exhaled. Impatience settled into his bouncing foot. "What do you have, Dak?"

Miller pointed at the monitors. "You can see her leaving in this shot from the ER, and over here you can see them head toward the back doors."

"That's it?" Adam drew in a lungful of air through his nose. Heat stirred in his gut and spread throughout his body.

"No, there's one more view." Miller tapped a few keys on the keyboard. "Here, you can see them in the employee parking lot. And that is all we have."

Ryker spoke, "Can we go through them again? Can you split the screen?"

"Of course."

Reviewing the footage again made Adam's stomach free-fall. The damp basement wrapped around him and suffocated his thoughts.

Not one shot of the man's face.

Ryker leaned closer to the monitor. "Can you tell where they went after they crossed the parking lot?"

"No, sir."

"That's The Evergreens on the other side of the trees," Ryker said.

"Correct. The Evergreen Ranch Homes."

"The Evergreens. Maybe someone with a security camera caught her or the vehicle leaving." Ryker pulled out his phone and requested uniforms to canvass the neighborhood for Jenny.

"Dak, is there any footage from when this guy came into the hospital?" Adam asked while he watched Jenny's frightened eyes stare up at him on the screen.

Hold on, baby, I'll find you.

"I'm sorry, no."

"How did he get in here, and not a single camera picked him up? And what does he want with Jenny?"

Ryker turned and faced Miller and leaned back beside the monitors. "How far back in time did you look? We don't know when this guy entered. He may have entered from another entrance."

The room filled with the crescendo of Dak's ringtone. "Miller . . . here?"

Adam turned and faced him, tracking every move he made.

"In the ER? . . . On the way." Dak disconnected. "Jenny was just brought into the ER—"

Adam tore out of the security office, raced down the hall, and bolted up the stairs, two at a time, Ryker and Dak on his heels.

Flying through the doors, Adam stopped, but the air in his lungs continued the sprint; his vision darkened except to see Jenny on the gurney being wheeled into the ER. Motionless, except for the rocking of the gurney that jostled her. Mascara streaked her pale cheeks, covered in scratches. The bottoms of her pants were torn and her sneakers muddy. More scratches covered her arms.

Adam went to her and took a hold of her hand. He lightly traced around her bruised wrist, then carefully turned her hand over and cradled both her wrists and inspected them. They had been rubbed raw, torn up like a piece of ground meat.

His blood simmered and heated to a rolling boil as he noticed more signs of a struggle.

Tenderly brushing her hair away from her face, Adam leaned down and rested his forehead against hers.

A nurse approached. "I'm sorry, sir. You'll have to wait in the waiting area until the doctor examines her."

"I'm not leaving."

"Sir—"

"I'm her husband." Adam lightly kissed her forehead.

"Adam." Nurse Greene gently rubbed Adam's back. "Let the doctors do their job. As soon as we know something, we'll come get you."

He gave her another kiss on her temple. "I'll be here, Boo, waiting."

Back again. Second time tonight.

The activity in the ER helped him slip in through the main ER entrance. No one gave him a second look. He rubbed his face, glad he'd ditched the scraggly beard.

As he hummed, his fingers tapped the melody on his thigh.

The thrill of the chase excited him, but most of all, he loved getting what he wanted.

A distraught man was creating the perfect distraction. The man making the scene halted his steps. It was the cop he'd noticed when he slipped in last night. There was no way he was still here for the drunk he'd brought in earlier.

The man was upset and said something to a nurse. He made out the word "husband."

The doors behind the cop opened, and that's when he recognized the pretty blonde nurse.

They found her. He knew they would. The corners of his lips curled. Nothing made him happier than when his plans went like they were supposed to.

He tugged down the bill of his ball cap and casually made his way to the doors that led to the records room. Looking over his shoulder, no one noticed him.

"Thank you, 'husband.'"

The access pad greeted him, and he swiped the employee card. "Thank you, Jennifer Taylor," he said to himself, and slipped into the room.

He flipped his burner cell open and dialed the number from memory. "I'm in."

"Get to a computer and put the flash drive in."

A few minutes later, he was accessing the files. "I owe you."

"Yes, you do."

He knew she wouldn't use her married name. His name. He tried her maiden name. Nothing. Did she think she could really get away from him? Did she really think he wouldn't track her down? No one walked away from him.

If they lived, it was because he let them.

He searched for the one thing he knew would tell him if she had been there. Three people came up who had visited the hospital in the last month with epilepsy. One was male, one was a sixty-five-year-old female, and a twenty-nine-year-old woman. She was seen just last week.

He clicked on the patient file, and her picture came up. She was stunning, and she was his. And now he knew where to find her and the name she was using.

Before he pulled out the flash drive, he typed in one more name: Richard Bennett. Reading through his file, he wrote down his listed address. One more glance at the screen and he noted Bennett's next of kin: Jennifer Taylor, sister. Parents deceased.

"Oh, darlin', get ready for our next date." A dark, slick grin slid into place.

A phone number lit up the display on his burner, and his grin evaporated. "What?"

"Now, is that how you talk to your employer, Slater? You don't sound happy to hear from me."

"I'm working." Slater folded the piece of paper with his wife's and Rick's information on it.

"Good. Does that mean you found my shipment?" Slater could feel Robert's beady little eyes through the phone.

"No. Soon, Robert." Slater tucked the paper away in his pocket.

"Work faster. If I have to come up there myself—"

"You'll get it. I gave you my word."

Robert growled, "You're running out of time. Did you find Rick?"

"I will."

"You need to move faster, Slater," he ordered.

"Give me a little more time."

"I'm not paying you for time."

"Trust me."

"You would sell your grandmother for a price."

"My grandmother is dead."

"That wouldn't stop you."

Slater snapped the disposable phone shut. The muscle behind his carotid knotted as his pulse thudded. Closing his eyes, he took a deep, soul-cleansing breath and let his thoughts return to being reunited with his wife . . . and what he had planned for Rick.

His smile returned.

Powering off the computer, he pulled his ball cap down, slipped out of the records department, and closed the door behind him. Another hallway leading to the main lobby of the hospital took Slater away from the ER.

The lobby was empty at this hour. With his head down, he slipped into the unmanned information booth. A portrait that hung behind the desk in the booth caught his eye. The pretty little nurse from earlier stared at him, smiling. And she was next to Ricky-boy. The plaque under the framed picture read, "In loving memory of Dr. Alan Carver Bennett."

He pulled out his phone and snapped a picture. Taking Jenny's access card from his pocket, he held it up next to her in the portrait. Younger, but definitely her. He snapped another picture.

He wiped off Jenny's card and laid it on the desk, whistling as he made his way out of the hospital.

Three

"What do you mean? I'm her husband!" Adam's pulse roared in his ears. He slammed through the doors—they slammed into the wall and rattled as they bounced off.

"Sir, you can't go back there. I'm going to get security," a nurse called after Adam.

The rooms blurred as they went by until he found Jenny's room.

Monitors beeped. Dim overhead lights cast a yellow glow over her complexion. Frail and small lying in the bed. "Oh, Boo," slipped out in a murmur.

"Adam." Dak Miller quietly spoke behind him.

"I'm not leaving." Adam stepped into Jenny's room. "You'll have to remove me."

Why do I have to keep reminding everyone that I'm her husband?

The bed rail was cool to his touch. He pulled a chair close to her and lowered the rail. He wrapped his hand around hers and sat next to her.

The toxicology report should be back soon, and no one could keep it from him. Nothing would stop him from working her case. He may not understand why Jenny wanted to divorce him, but he was determined not to make it easy for her.

"Whoever did this to you will pay, Jenny. I promise. I will find them and bring them to justice." Adam gently brushed her hair from her cheek and ran his thumb down the side of her face.

A rap sounded on the doorframe, and Adam braced himself. "I'm not leaving, Miller."

"Good. I'm not asking you to leave." Drew Collins stood in the doorway, hands in his front pockets. "Ryker asked me to check on you and get an update on Jenny."

Adam leaned back. He rubbed circles with his thumb on the back of Jenny's hand. "No change."

Drew stepped into the room, and at the foot of the bed, his gaze rested on Jenny. "I'm sorry, man. How you holding up?"

Adam worked his jaw back and forth and blew out a breath. "How am I holding up? Let's see. My wife is lying in a hospital bed and she won't wake up. No one knows why. She wants to divorce me. I have no idea why. She's been trying to for months, and her reasons are unfounded. Tonight, I find out she's removed me as her next of kin from her medical records, so no one is supposed to talk to me about what's going on with her."

Adam fished his badge out of his pocket. "It's a good thing I have this, and I'm investigating her kidnapping because it's the only way I'm going to get answers." He looked at Jenny and took her hand once more. "One thing I do know is that any answers I get won't come from my own wife."

Adam leaned forward and rested his head on the bed. A sigh escaped, and he rolled his head to the side to meet Drew's gaze. "Sorry." He sagged back in the chair again. "I didn't mean to dump all that on you."

"It's okay. But since we still don't know what happened, I'll be staying outside tonight. Boss's orders."

"Thank you, man. But let a uniform do it. You're a detective now."

"Let's just say you'll owe me one."

Gurneys rushed past. Nurses scrambled on the heels of doctors.

Drew leaned on the wall outside Jenny's room. He'd take police work any day. But these men and women were true heroes.

A shudder twisted through him at the too-many memories of broken bones and trips to the ER as a kid.

A nurse approached, and he moved his muscular frame in front of Jenny's door.

"Excuse me," the nurse said and took a step back.

"Credentials, please." Drew held out his hand.

"Since when?" She arched an eyebrow at Drew.

"Since Mrs. Taylor's life was threatened tonight. Now, may I see your credentials, please?"

She eyed him for a moment, then pulled her badge off her sweater and smacked her ID into his big palm.

He inspected it, both sides of the badge, then held the badge next to her.

Her fists flew to her round hips. "Is there a problem?"

"Just trying to see if this is really you. You're actually smiling in this picture."

She snatched her ID back and clipped it on her sweater.

The nurse crossed her arms over her chest. Her gaze skimmed over Drew from head to toe. "How do I know you're really here to watch Mrs. Taylor? You're kind of brutish." She stood a little straighter, a little stiffer. "Where are your credentials?"

Drew didn't budge. Inwardly, he winced at being under her scrutiny. Reaching into his back pocket, he pulled out his identification and flipped it open toward the nurse.

She reached up and plucked it from his fingers. Surprise crossed her face before she could hide it. "Nice picture. You might want to look into updating it."

Drew held out his hand. She sucked in her lips, trying to stop her giggle, and set his credentials in the palm of his hand. He stepped aside and allowed her access to Jenny's room. He shook his head and stood against the wall. The next time he was at the station, he was updating his rookie picture.

A few minutes later, she came out. "Thank you," she said as she went down the hall.

A sweet dream wove through Jenny, warming every inch of her. A lazy smile graced her face. She rolled to her side and her eyes flickered open.

Adam. Always there for her. Always made her feel safe. Contentment and peace wrapped around her like a favorite blanket.

He couldn't be comfortable. His blond hair tumbled over his forehead, begging for her to run her fingers through it and brush it back into place.

Her eyes darted open, and she jerked up into a sitting position. The IV port pulled on her hand, and the stand clanged when it smacked into the bed frame. Her hand throbbed. Sweat broke out on Jenny's back like she'd run circles around the hospital.

What happened? Why is Adam here?

"Adam. Adam, wake up."

He unfolded himself and stretched. "Hey, you're awake. How do you feel?"

"Why are you here? You're not supposed to be here." Jenny's voice rose with each word that tumbled out. "What have they told you?" she hissed.

Adam's shoulders sagged, and he dropped his head. He let out a long and very visible sigh; his whole body seemed to deflate. "We don't really know much, Jen. We know you weren't sexually assaulted, and the toxicology report that came back last night showed you had propofol in your system."

"Oh—"

The hospital room door flew open. "I heard what happened and came right away." A petite woman rushed through the door.

Drew followed her into the room. "I'm sorry. She pushed past me. I can remove her if you'd like."

Jenny sat up. "No, that won't be necessary."

"I can see with her imposing size why you couldn't stop her." Adam mocked Drew with a fake shiver.

"Hey, I may be small, but I'm mighty," she protested, and scowled at Adam.

"Adam, this is Bethany," Jenny said.

Bethany rushed over and hugged Jenny. "I was so worried. I came as soon as I heard."

Adam stood and crossed his arms. "Bethany . . . from your attorney's office, Bethany?"

"Yes, sir." Bethany's bracelets jingled when she stretched her arm across Jenny's bed to shake Adam's hand.

Adam studied Bethany's offered hand. "Under different circumstances, I'm sure it would be a pleasure to meet you." He took her hand and shook it.

"Jenny, I still need to ask you some questions about last night."

"Now? Can I have a minute with Bethany?"

Adam eyed Bethany. "Sure. I could use some coffee." He hesitated at the door and glanced back at Jenny. "For what it's worth, I'm glad you're okay."

After the door closed, Bethany looked at Jenny. "Why are you divorcing that man?" She jerked her head toward the door Adam just went through.

"It's complicated." Sheets and blankets balled in Jenny's fist.

"Well, he still loves you. It's written all over his face." Bethany tapped her chin with a coral-polished nail. "And I think you're still in love with him."

Everything inside of Jenny screamed and begged for her to run after Adam. "You don't know that, and it doesn't matter."

"Oh, yes it does. Love will get you through whatever is going on between you guys."

"Ever think it's because I love him I'm doing this?"

Bethany gave a small nod. "As your friend and not just the paralegal helping you, that's the dumbest thing I've ever heard."

Jenny's eyes narrowed into tiny slits at Bethany. "Does Uncle Edward know you're here?"

"No, why? Did something happen?" Bethany walked around Jenny's bed and took the seat Adam had been sitting in.

"You mean more than what put me here in a hospital bed? No, nothing else happened."

"I came here for you. I was worried." Bethany latched on to Jenny's hand.

"I'm sorry. Seeing Adam is harder than I thought."

Bethany tilted her head. "Uh-huh. Because you still love him."

Jenny hated herself, but she was certain she was doing the right thing. She just had to convince everyone else.

Bethany gave her hand a squeeze and asked, "Do you need anything? Is there anything I can do for you? Do they know what happened? Have they caught the guy who did this?"

Jenny chuckled at the onslaught of questions. "The toxicology report came in last night. Adam said I had propofol in my system. I feel fine."

Bethany moved to sit on the bed next to Jenny and gave her another hug.

"I'm fine, really," Jenny said, as Bethany squeezed the air out of her.

"Do they know who took you?"

"Not that I know of, but I haven't had a lot of time to find out. I'm concerned, though."

"Why?"

"Adam is working my case."

Bethany tilted her head again. "Why is that a problem? You yourself said he's a brilliant detective, and we both know he loves you."

"Stop saying that."

"What? That he's a brilliant detective?"

"No, that he loves me."

"Oh, honey, he does."

"Focus, Bethany. If Adam is going to be working this case, I don't want him snooping around where I don't want him snooping."

"You know, you never told me why you're divorcing him."

"I know."

Drew pushed the door open and moved out of the way. Adam walked back into the room and set a cup of coffee on the table for Jenny and offered one to Bethany with a couple of creams and sugar packets. "I didn't know how you took your coffee."

Bethany smirked at Jenny, and Jenny wanted to dive under the covers and never come out.

"Thank you. That's very thoughtful of you." An I-told-you-so grin broke out, and she turned back to Jenny and gave her a quick kiss on the cheek. "I'm going to take my coffee and leave you. You call me if you need anything. Anything at all. Got it?"

"Yes."

"Promise?"

"Yes, I promise."

She saluted Adam with her coffee. "Thank you, and it was nice meeting you." Bethany gathered the rest of her things and left.

"She cares about you."

"She's become a good friend. What did you find out about last night?" Jenny's eyes followed Adam as he took the seat Bethany just vacated.

Coffee in one hand, he reached for Jenny. She scooted back.

"Adam, what did you find out?"

A long sigh pushed past his lips. "We reviewed all the hospital's footage from last night, and we don't have much to go on. Once you left the parking lot, we don't know what happened. Uniforms are still canvassing the neighborhood on the other side of the woods, hoping someone either saw something or caught something on their security cameras."

"How did I get here?"

"You were found in a car at the entrance of a county service road. Maintenance personnel found you when they were trying to leave for the night."

"I don't even know where I was or where we were going last night." Jenny grasped the blanket, her knuckles white.

"Thankfully, whoever left you knew that someone would be coming. Well, I'm assuming. The car you were in was blocking their exit, so they had no choice but to call for help and help you."

"Why was I taken?"

Sitting down his coffee, Adam reached into his pocket and pulled out Jenny's hospital ID card in an evidence bag. The bag crinkled when he passed it to her. "We think he was after this."

She turned it over in her hand. "Why?"

"We have footage of a guy in a ball cap leaving this on the desk in the volunteer station early this morning. Tech is checking what your ID was used to access."

Jenny smoothed the evidence bag against her badge. "Adam, I don't understand. Why me?"

He studied her for a moment. "At first, we didn't think it was personal. We thought it was a crime of opportunity."

"At first?"

Adam leaned forward and took Jenny's hand in a firm grip. "Jenny, before he left the hospital, we see him snapping a picture of the family portrait that hangs behind the desk in the lobby. Then he holds up your ID next to you in the portrait and snaps another picture."

"But he left my ID." Jenny's voice shook with fear weaving its way through her mind.

"Also, the man who took you doesn't resemble the man who used your badge—at all."

Jenny pulled out of Adam's grip. Her chin wobbled, and her voice lowered to a whisper. "What do you mean? The man last night was disheveled and dirty. His car smelled. He said he was going to kill me."

Adam scooted closer. "Honey, I need you to tell me everything you remember. What happened when I last saw you and Nurse Greene asked you to check on the other patient?"

"No," she squeaked out, then cleared her throat and tried again. "No."

"No? What do you mean, no?" Adam sat a little taller with his forearms leaning on the chair's armrests.

Jenny closed her eyes and took a slow, deep breath. When she opened them, she looked at the twisted blanket around her fingers, not Adam. "You can't work this case, my case. I won't allow it."

Adam stood, leaned on the bed rail, and bent over Jenny. "Jenny, I am working your case."

"No, you're not."

Four

The drive home from the hospital blurred in Jenny's rearview. She sat in her car and stared at the garage door. The last thing she wanted to do was go into that shell of a home.

She rubbed the diamond in her engagement ring with her thumb. The same questions rolled around her mind. Why did she get sick? Why did God allow it? Why wasn't God making her better?

Rings that represented a future with the man she thought she'd be with forever slid into her palm. Her fingers closed over them. She didn't want to let him go, but what choice did she have? She was doing the right thing. A tear spilled down her cheek. She slipped her rings back on as easily as they'd slipped off.

Her MINI Cooper rocked when she slammed the door. Walking up the steps to her front door was like walking in molasses—slow and making little progress. As she trudged up the steps, the house's shadow swallowed her. Washed-out yellow siding and a drab burgundy door taunted her. The white trim had weathered and cracked. A house that was once filled with love, laughter, and dreams was now a reminder of what she'd never have again.

Tears streamed down her cheeks, and her hands trembled.

The key refused to slide into the lock. She smacked the door.

Adam must hate me. I hate me.

The dead bolt slipped into place when she finally unlocked the door. A chilly, drafty home devoid of life was all that waited for her. Long shifts kept her from facing the memories that greeted her every time she walked through the door. When Adam signed the papers, she'd sell.

Tears soaked Jenny's sleeve as she wiped them away. Keys clanked off each other when she tossed them and her purse onto the couch. She nudged the door closed with her heel, flipped on the lamp, and shed her sweater—wadded it up and tossed it on top of the mess she left on the couch. She turned toward the alarm pad, but it wasn't set. After Friday, she'd been careful to set it. She gave the keypad a one-shoulder shrug. "Guess I forgot," Jenny said to no one.

A tension headache nudged its way up the base of her neck. The scrubs she wore told the story of her twelve-hour shift. The first one since she'd been abducted last Friday. She was glad to be back to full shifts, but all she wanted now was a shower, some clean clothes, and the gallon of peanut-butter-ripple ice cream in her freezer to drown out her conscience.

Her fingers kneaded her temples, and she walked down the dark hallway to her bedroom.

The room lit up like an airport runway when she flipped on the lights. Jenny shielded her eyes and clutched the doorjamb to stop her steps. She turned the overhead lights off and turned on the correct light by the bed. Jenny gave her eyes a minute to adjust before she stepped into the room.

The first step into the room stopped her cold.

Blood. Blood that trailed on the carpet back out and down the same hallway she'd just come down.

A shaky hand flew to her mouth. Bile rose, and she swallowed it back down.

She followed the trail and tracked it back to the front door.

How did I miss this?

She scanned the room, grabbed a candlestick holder off the dining room table, and held it high above her head. With slow, deliberate steps, she walked back to her bedroom, careful to step over the blood on the floor. Standing next to her bed, her eyes swept the room. One word squeezed out of her tight, strained throat, "Adam?"

A groan filled the room, and Jenny whirled around. A man's frame filled the doorway and slouched on the doorframe. Shadows covered his face. She took a step closer and sucked in air when her eyes connected with eyes like her own.

The candlestick thudded to the floor, and Jenny ran to her brother. "Rick! What happened?"

He swayed and stepped into the bedroom, then slumped into Jenny's arms.

She led him over to her bed, and he dropped like an anvil. Blood covered the front of him. She reached out and slid her hand under his jacket. Warm blood covered her hand as she peeled back his jacket. "Rick, what happened?" Blood oozed out of the wound in his shoulder. "I'll be right back."

Jenny ran to the master bath and rummaged through the linen closet and medicine cabinet, grabbing towels and supplies.

She tore his shirt open and took a closer look at the wound. *This can't be happening. I can't lose my brother too.* Jenny forced herself into nurse mode. She palpated the wound, then applied pressure to it.

He winced.

"Rick, what happened? How did this happen?" She applied more pressure to stop the flow of blood.

Through a tight jaw, Rick said, "It doesn't matter. Can you fix it?" His breathing was shallow and labored. "Come on, Jen, I know you can."

Her lips thinned. "Don't I always fix it?"

"Jen, please. I need your help." Rick wiped the sweat off his forehead with the back of his hand, smearing blood across it.

"You may have damaged your rotator cuff or worse." Jenny reached for another towel. "Rick, tell me what's going on?"

His voice quivered, and he shook his head. "Just sew me up, okay?"

"Come on. You owe me that much."

"It's nothing, I promise." Rick tried to sit up.

Jenny shoved him back down. "I need you to stay still. If you don't stop moving, I'll sew you to the bed. You need stitches. I've got to get you to the hospital."

"No! No hospitals. You can do it. I know you can. Please, Jen."

"Who did this to you, Rick?"

Rick's eyes widened and darted around the room. "Where's Adam?"

"I don't know, work, I guess," Jenny's reply came out short and terse.

"When will he be home?"

"He doesn't live here anymore, remember? We're getting a divorce. That hasn't changed." It would be nice if her only sibling cared enough to remember what was going on in her life. Boston was looking better and better.

"Jen, listen. Please. I need to get out of here."

"What's going on, Rick?" Jenny ran back to her bathroom for more supplies.

"Just fix me up." Rick jumped as she dumped antiseptic on his wound. "Does that have to hurt so much?"

"Do you want an infection?" She leaned down and got in his face and enunciated every word. "Stay still."

"I can't stay here."

"You're bleeding too much." Jenny fought to keep her voice even.

"If you can't stitch it up, then do you have any of those butterfly things you used to use when we were kids?" he said with short, pained gulps of air.

"Rick, this needs to be packed, and you need stitches. How many times do I have to tell you? You might even need surgery."

He grabbed her hands. "Stop, Jen. Look at me."

She met his gaze and sat back on the bed.

"I'm sorry. I messed up again, but I can't go to the hospital. I need to get out of here. Please help me." His words were raw and rough.

"Rick, you need help. And not just stitches. Is it gambling again or drugs? Are you in trouble?" Her eyes searched his for answers.

"The less you know, the better. Please. I really need to get out of here."

Gravel crunched under the wheels of Adam's SUV as it came to a stop. Dusk began to settle over Otter Bay. Streetlights up and down the street came on, fighting the darkness moving in. Shadows danced across perfectly manicured lawns, overgrown lawns, and lawns littered with bikes and balls.

"Maybe this time would be different," Adam said as he pushed open his door, and stepped onto the street. Dread pooled in his gut. His steps heavy.

Jenny's electric-blue MINI Cooper convertible sat in their driveway. Soon to be her driveway.

The screen door flung open with a little more force than he'd intended and smacked the house. He reached for the handle, then stopped. He should knock and not be a clod and go barging in even if it was still his house too.

He reached for the handle again. A grin crept across his face when he rubbed the nick in the doorframe where it'd met their dresser when they moved in. A day he'd never forget:

"Boo, where's the box cutter?"

"On the counter in the kitchen."

"I don't remember us having all this stuff in the apartment. Where were you stashing it?"

"My parents' garage," Jenny had hollered from another room.

Adam looked around the kitchen and sighed. They needed a bigger house already.

A knock on the door pulled him from his thoughts. "Can I help you?"

"Taylor residence?"

Adam raised an eyebrow at the man at his door. "Yes."

"Bay Electronics. Delivering your"—the man looked down at his clipboard—"TV and rock speakers and R2D2 dehumidifier." The man looked at Adam again. "There must be a mistake. I'm sorry."

Jenny came around the corner. "No mistake. The speakers are his, and the dehumidifier is mine."

The man hesitated, then looked between the two of them and nodded.

Adam placed an arm around Jenny and mocked wiping a tear from under his eye. "I've never been prouder. I don't think you could have confused that poor man any more if you'd tried."

Jenny swatted him. "Don't you have a box to unpack?"

"Millions of them . . ." Adam said as he rolled his eyes.

About an hour later, Adam called out to Jenny, "Boo, are you ready for a break? I could use one."

When she didn't answer back, he went searching for her.

He found her asleep on some boxes with packing peanuts stuck to her cheek and chin. She had worked the night shift and swore she didn't need to rest or nap. Her body had told a different story.

She was so beautiful. The rhythm of her breathing was quiet and steady. Hair that had fallen out of her ponytail, wisped across her jaw and neck.

He walked over and tenderly scooped her up and carried her into their new bedroom. She snuggled into him, and he knew . . .

He was home.

"Was that a car door?" Rick said as he pushed up off the bed and teetered. He fell and tumbled against the dresser; Jenny's things scattered and crashed to the floor.

"Stay still. Let me finish this, please." Jenny grabbed his arm and tried to pull him back down.

Rick found his footing. "I have to go." Rick ambled his way around Jenny and grabbed the ibuprofen off the nightstand. "I'll go out the slider." His breath was still labored.

"Rick, please. Let me finish," she pleaded.

He leaned down and kissed her on the cheek. "I'll be fine."

"Rick, wait!"

He paused at the slider and looked back at Jenny. "I love you. Don't you forget that. Ever."

"I love you too," she said as he disappeared out the door.

Adam shook his head and rapped his knuckles on the door. It opened with the first tap.

"Jenny, you here?" A chill climbed through Adam, leaving the hairs on the back of his neck to stand on end.

He took a step into the room, and his eyes swept over the space. The living room hadn't changed. Jenny hadn't changed a thing.

Drops of blood on the floor that trailed toward the hall caught his attention. Adam pulled out his Sig Sauer 9mm and followed the blood. "Jenny, honey, you here?"

Adam followed the trail down the hall. "Boo, where are you?"

Light from the master bedroom spilled into the hallway through the open door. He slowed his steps, kept his gun at the ready position, and pressed his body against the wall.

He glanced around the doorframe; Jenny's back was to him, standing over the bed, her shoulders hunched.

Adam forced his voice to be even and soothing. "Jenny, is everything okay?"

She jumped and turned, thrusting her hands behind her back.

"Jenny, step away from the bed." Adam made his way into the room, taking cautious steps until he was standing next to her, next to the bed.

"Adam, why are you here?" Jenny wormed herself between Adam and the bed. She reached behind and picked up the towel—never breaking eye contact with Adam.

"What's going on, Jen?" Adam stepped back, his gaze running along the trail of blood from the bathroom to the bed to the bloody towel in front of the slider.

"Nothing."

"Don't tell me nothing. This is not a paper cut," he said, pointing to the blood on the bed.

"It's nothing, really."

He turned and took a step toward the bathroom. He glanced back before he went in. The contents of the medicine cabinet littered the counter, and towels from the linen closet scattered over the floor. He walked over to the shower and pulled back the curtain. Empty. He went back to the bedroom and searched the closet. "I need to call this in."

Jenny's head jerked up. "No, don't! Please, Adam, you can't."

"Jenny, you're covered in blood. There is a trail of blood from the front door to the bedroom. I have to call it in." Adam's gaze traveled over the room again. "Who else is in the house?"

"No one. I swear." Jenny's right hand shot up like she was testifying in court.

Adam stared down at his wife, and with slow and deliberate words, said, "Whose blood is that? Who was here?"

Jenny held his gaze, then wrapped the towel she was still holding around both of her hands.

"It's still my house, a cop's house. Are you asking me to look the other way?"

She continued to stare up at him and chewed on her bottom lip.

"I can't, Jenny. Tell me what happened?" Adam broke eye contact and scanned the room again.

He walked over to the slider. Tension crept into his shoulders like a rubber band that was stretched too far and getting ready to snap. "There's blood on the handle."

"I just closed the door," Jenny said, as she held up her hand again.

"Whose blood is this? Tell me what happened, or I'm calling it in."

"I can't." She looked away and mumbled, "I'm sorry." An errant tear ran down her cheek.

"Wait. It was Rick, wasn't it?" Adam stowed his gun and brought his six-foot-one muscular frame to its full height. He dragged a frustrated hand through his blond hair before settling it on his hip. "What happened? And what did he want this time?"

Jenny's face blanched. "That's not fair."

"When does Rick not want something? I have to call this in. You know there's a warrant out for him." Adam pulled out his phone. "Did you give him any money?"

Jenny ran over to Adam and stepped in front of him. She reached up for his phone. "Please, Adam. Let it go."

"Don't put me in this position. I will not lose my job because of Rick. I won't protect him."

"What about me? What happens to me when they find out he was here and I didn't call the police?"

Five

The ocean mirrored bands of yellow and shades of purple that streaked over the horizon as the sun crested the water's edge. The lighthouse's long shadow clung to the seaside. Adam's steps pounded down the trail, and he raced up the bluffs, pushing himself faster and faster.

He had to get his head on straight if he was going to help Jenny. He couldn't let anyone get inside his head—not Jenny, not Rick.

Jenny needed him, even if she wouldn't admit it.

And he needed to find Rick. Adam had to know what went on last night. If all that was Rick's blood, where was he? Did Jenny know where he was? Was she keeping Rick from him? Did she give him money . . . again?

Did Rick have anything to do with Jenny being taken from the hospital? Of course he did. When was Rick ever innocent? Rick had always been a problem and an even bigger problem in their marriage.

He continued to push himself down the trail, kicking up gravel with each step. Water quietly lapped the bank, only disturbed by the pebbles tossed in with each long stride Adam used to propel himself forward.

Crossing over the apex of the trail, Adam saw a motorcycle with a man bent over it, inspecting the engine. Adam slowed his pace until he reached the motorcyclist. "Good morning. Do you need a hand?"

The man stood and wiped greased on his jeans. "No. I'm fine. Thank you."

"Looks like you're having some trouble," Adam said as he regulated his breathing from his run.

"It sticks. She's a project."

Adam swallowed his laugh. "Her?"

The man dipped his chin toward Adam and straddled the bike. He slipped his helmet and gloves back on, then started the bike, saluted Adam, and took off.

As the man pulled away onto the road, Adam's gut knotted with unease that coiled his insides.

"Have you completely lost your mind?" Ryker stood in front of his desk, facing Adam's desk.

Adam looked up, eyebrows high, and laid the report he was reading on his desk. "What?"

"What do you mean, what? You arrested Jenny?"

"No." Adam stood, placed his fists on his desk as he leaned on it.

Ryker crossed his arms over his chest. "I thought you were trying to win her back. I thought you didn't want the divorce. You could not have done anything dumber."

Adam looked down at his desk, closed his eyes, and exhaled. "I didn't arrest Jenny."

"What you did was stupid." Ryker held his stance.

"What was I supposed to do?" Adam stood and crossed his arms, mirroring Ryker.

"Not arrest her."

"You mean not do my job? Besides, I wasn't the arresting officer."

"No, you weren't, but you called it in, and you had a uniform come out and do it for you. Your name may not be on the report, but it's thanks to you she was almost put in handcuffs."

"She was aiding and abetting her brother." Heat inched up Adam's neck.

"You feel she chose her brother over you."

"What am I supposed to think?" Adam's voice rose with each word. Heads in the bullpen turned their way.

"Clearly you weren't." Ryker huffed out.

"What would you have done? Would you look the other way if Amanda had information on a case? Would you not uphold the law if Amanda was hiding something or someone?"

"I would like to stay married, which is what I thought you wanted."

"I do want to stay married." Adam arched an eyebrow in a challenge. "You're avoiding my questions."

Ryker unfolded his arms and took his chair. "Fine. I would not arrest Amanda for withholding information."

"Oh, isn't that rich? Doesn't that break some Bible code or something?"

"Adam, look, man, if I were in your shoes, I would not have arrested Jenny. You know she doesn't have any information about her brother. She hasn't for a long time. He shows up when he needs something, then disappears again."

"I know. I'm sick of it, and I'm sick of her protecting him." Adam's head sank below his shoulders, and he returned to his own chair. The wheels squeaked as he rolled toward his desk.

"Arresting her wasn't the way to show her."

"Nothing has worked with her." Adam grabbed ahold of his desk and pulled himself the rest of the way.

"Give it time."

"I'm tired of waiting."

"So where is Jenny now?"

Adam shifted his gaze to the whiteboard and talked to the board. "How would I know? She's not talking to me."

Ryker blew out a frustrated breath and tossed his keys and phone onto his blotter. He scrubbed his hands over his face. "Did tech figure out what Jenny's hospital ID was used for?"

Adam picked up the report he had been reading. "Not that I know. I haven't heard from them." He compared the report to his computer screen. "Do you recognize the name Cole Slater?"

"No. Should I?"

"Maybe not." Adam gave a slight shrug. "When I was on my run this morning, I ran into him. Something felt off. Odd. I've never seen him before."

"Get used to it. Our little town is growing." Ryker looked up. "Wait. How do you know this guy's name?"

"He seemed *off*." Adam continued to study his computer screen. "I ran his plates."

One of Ryker's eyebrows rose. "Did you run his name?"

"Ran his name and plates, and I haven't found a thing." Adam leaned back in his chair with his fingers laced behind his head. "We need a lead. Jenny's attacker is out there."

Adam faced the whiteboard again. He pivoted in his chair back to his computer and closed the search on Cole Slater. Picking up the reports and pictures, he laid them out on his desk. There had to be a connection somewhere.

A file folder appeared with a smack on his desk in front of him. "Tech asked me to drop this off," Drew Collins said.

Adam tore into the envelope and yanked the report free.

Ryker leaned forward. "What's it say?"

"It says her ID was used to enter the records room." Adam turned the paper over and shook it.

"That's it?"

"That's it." He released the paper like it was on fire and watched it float to his desk. "That doesn't help much."

"What was accessed?" Drew asked.

"They weren't able to see that. They just know which computer was used."

Drew took a seat next to Adam's desk and held his hand out. "Can I see that?"

Adam passed the report to him. "It doesn't say much."

"No, but we can at least figure out how long this guy was in the records room between when he used Jenny's ID and the timestamp from security, when we see him leaving her ID on the volunteer's desk."

Adam shuffled some papers around and found the report he was looking for. "Security has this guy leaving the hospital at two forty-three a.m."

"This report says Jenny's ID entered the records room at two twenty-seven a.m. He wasn't in there long. I'm guessing he found what he was looking for and got out of there." Drew handed the report back to Adam and went over to the whiteboard and added the new information. He tapped his chin with the capped marker as he studied the board. "What have we found out about this guy?"

Ryker joined him at the board. "Nothing. We're not even sure they're the same guy. It could be more than one, and they're working together."

Drew gave his head a small shake. "My money says it's the same guy."

Adam joined them. "Based on?"

"Because he's after something. Jenny is still alive, and her hospital ID was returned." Drew pointed to the picture on the board of the family portrait where the man held Jenny's ID next to her. "I don't think he knew her before he took her. Can I look at the footage from the lobby?"

Drew sat down in front of Adam's computer and pulled up the video from the hospital lobby. Drew replayed the video over and over at different speeds. "There," he said, tapping the screen in front of him.

Adam leaned over Drew's shoulder. "Where?"

Ryker joined them. "What are we looking at? We can't see the guy's face."

Drew glanced at Ryker. "No, you can't. But watch." He slowed down the video and replayed it.

"What am I supposed to be seeing?" Adam hissed out.

Ryker shot Adam a look that said *knock it off.*

Drew played the video again and slowed it down further when the man saw the portrait, and recognition hit him when he saw Rick. "Did you see it?" Drew looked between Adam and Ryker. "The slight nod. It's there, but you have to be looking for it. He recognized Rick."

"You can't know that." Ryker straightened and studied the whiteboard.

Adam stepped back and began to wear a hole in the linoleum. "If Rick has anything to do with what happened to Jenny, I'll kill him."

Drew played the video a few more times. "I think Jenny was in the wrong place at the wrong time."

"Well, Rick is always in the wrong place at all the wrong times," Adam said as he reclaimed his seat.

"I hate to go, but I have to take Amanda to her doctor's appointment. I'll be back. Don't do anything until I get back. Got it?" Ryker zeroed in on Adam.

"Sure."

"I mean it. Don't leave this station."

"Fine." Adam tore himself from the video and grinned like a Cheshire cat at Ryker. "How's Amanda and the baby?"

Ryker's face lit up like a kid at Christmas. Adam knew he would be a good dad. "They are both doing great. Amanda says I'm hovering." His huge smile took over. "And I don't intend to stop."

Adam replayed the video of the night Jenny was abducted. All he wanted was one good look of the man's face. The man was smart. He hid his face from all the cameras. Was Drew right? Was it only one, or were there two men involved?

The footage of Jenny's abduction from the hospital, and the footage of the man who accessed the records room, was as much as he was going to get unless someone came forward from one of the bordering neighborhoods. They had to be missing something. There had to be more footage.

Whoever breached the hospital records had to get into the hospital.

He opened the file folder on his desktop and scanned the security videos again. No file was timestamped around the time the records room was accessed.

They knew when the records room was accessed, and they knew what the man was wearing. Certainly, they could find out when and where this guy entered.

He dialed Dak Miller's cell phone. Voicemail. "Dak, I'm on my way over. I need to see some additional footage of the night Jenny was abducted. I'll explain when I get there."

Adam stood and reached for his jacket from the back of his chair.

"Have you found anything yet?" Captain Danvers asked as he walked over to Adam's desk.

"No, sir."

"Come to my office. We need to talk about Jenny's case." The captain nodded in the direction of his office and walked away.

When Adam arrived at his captain's office, he settled himself in the chair opposite him.

Captain Danvers sat down and rested his forearms on his desk. "This isn't easy."

"We're still reviewing footage from the neighbors and businesses close to the hospital."

"No, I mean, I'm sorry, Detective. I have to remove you from the case."

"Why?" Adam sat up higher and rubbed his palms down his thighs.

"You're too close to the case. I'm sorry." The captain leaned back in his chair, opening the file he'd been leaning on.

"You didn't remove Ryker when we were working Amanda's case." Not that long ago he and Ryker were working her case. Amanda's life was in danger, and nothing could have stopped Ryker from protecting her.

"You know we almost did, but he wasn't married to her at the time," he said, flipping through the file.

"Sir, I can be objective." The tension knot in his shoulders twisted. Rick flashed through his mind and Jenny's plea not to call in Rick being at their house last night.

"You know department policy. I will leave Detective Scott on the case, along with Detective Collins."

"Sir, I know Ryker and Drew are more than capable, but she's my wife."

"You're too close. Sometimes stepping back is the right thing to do."

Every time Adam thought he'd found a way to finally get answers, he hit a wall. "Captain, I can be objective. I promise, sir." He stretched out his hands and bent his fingers back, trying to get the feeling to return.

"Don't make me put you on desk duty or administrative leave. Do we need to talk about last night?"

"No, sir. But for the record, I did the right thing." Adam stood, and the chair toppled over. He righted it and turned back to Captain Danvers. "You know, I haven't taken a vacation in a long time. Now might be a good time to take one." The knot in his shoulders eased a bit as he made his way to the door.

"I don't want you working this case. You've also been banned from the hospital."

Adam stopped and turned around. "For what reason?"

"Ignoring Jenny's medical directives for her records. Refusing to leave when security asked you to. Should I go on?" Captain Danvers held up the complaint from the hospital.

Adam stood in the doorway and studied his captain. "If you were in my shoes, what would you do, sir?"

"If I thought Mia was in any kind of danger, I wouldn't leave her side. No one would get to her without going through me first."

Adam grabbed his keys off his desk and stalked through the department, heading for the door when he ran into Ryker.

"Where are you going?" Ryker stopped his forward progress with a hand to his chest.

"Looks like I'm out. It's you and boy genius." Adam took a step back and shrugged into his jacket.

"Captain talked to you?"

"You knew?" Adam said, adjusting his collar.

"He called on the way to Amanda's appointment."

"Right." Adam gave him a nod. "How's she doing?"

"She's fine. The baby is fine." He looked ten feet tall when he spoke about Amanda and the baby.

"Glad to hear."

"You didn't answer my question. Where are you going?"

"Vacation."

"Funny."

"I told you, I'm off Jenny's case, and I'm taking a vacation." Adam's step turned a little lighter as he walked out the door.

Ryker called after him. "Don't do anything you'll regret."

Six

"Everything looks good, Jenny." Dr. Laghari closed her file and rested his arms on it.

"Thank you. I just wanted to be sure." Jenny's fingers played with the cross that hung around her neck.

Dr. Laghari slid his chair back and walked around his desk. He took the empty seat next to Jenny and offered her his hand. His hand was warm and soft when she placed hers in his.

"Jenny, what's really going on? You and I both know if the propofol was going to cause you any problems, it would have happened while it was still in your system."

She sniffed and looked away. Dr. Laghari passed her a tissue.

"Sweetheart, you can talk to me. You know your dad and I were close, and I'd like to think you came to me because you trust me. What's going on?"

The man sitting next to her, she thought of like her own father. She knew she could trust him.

He knew her secret.

"I see you're wearing your mom's cross. Does that mean you're back at church?"

Jenny balled up the tissue. "I go when I can. Yes."

"I'm glad to hear that." Dr. Laghari pointed to Jenny's cross. "Did you know your dad gave that cross to your mom? They were in college and he wanted to get engaged. He couldn't afford an engagement ring. So he bought her that cross and told her Christ would always be with them and their marriage." Dr. Laghari held Jenny's hands again. "Jenny, God is always faithful; you can trust Him."

Jenny brushed the cross like she was getting wrinkles out of it. "I wish I understood more. I have so many questions about my parents' deaths and why God took them. I have so many questions about why I'm sick."

"We'll get through this."

"But we don't know the extent of its progression or the long-term effects it could have."

"No, we don't. I'm not ready to label your MS until we can see how remission goes. Let's take today and focus on today. How's the medication doing?"

Jenny gave a one-shoulder shrug. "My balance is still a problem. I don't know what to do about the tingling, the frequency of headaches, and I'm tired all the time." A chuckle slipped out. "Well, the propofol-induced sleep helped a little with the fatigue, but I'm still tired."

"Then let's look at other treatments."

"There's a lot going on. Maybe it's stress." She dabbed under her eye with the tissue.

"Do you want to wait for your next regular visit and talk about other treatments that are available? That will give us a little more time to see how you respond to your current treatment. You know you need to watch your stress."

Jenny nodded and blew her nose. She looked around for a trash can.

"By the door," Dr. Laghari said. "How's Adam doing with all of this? I'm sure he's happy to help."

Jenny retook her seat and looked down at the wedding ring on her finger. "We're getting a divorce."

When Dr. Laghari didn't respond, she glanced at him and saw disappointment in his eyes. "There is nothing I dislike more than a man who won't stand by his wife in a crisis or dealing with a long-term diagnosis." He stood and walked to his window overlooking the Charles River. "Did he really file for divorce?"

The room turned a hundred degrees warmer. "No . . . I did."

He turned back to Jenny. "Oh, Jenny, why? What happened?"

"He doesn't need to be saddled with this, with me."

"Oh, honey, that's not your call. God brought you two together. You need to trust Him. He knows what He's doing." Dr. Laghari sat next to Jenny again. "Have you prayed about it?"

"I don't need to."

"Yes, you do, sweetheart. You may be back in church, but a relationship with Jesus is so much more than showing up for church on Sunday."

"I know. I know. I'm trying."

"You're trying on your own. You have to be open to the support God has placed around you. Don't be afraid to accept help."

"I have you and the other medical personnel helping me."

"Is that what you tell your own patients?"

Jenny checked the time on the antique desk clock Dr. Laghari had sitting behind his desk on the credenza. She stood and hiked her purse strap over her shoulder. "I need to be going."

Dr. Laghari stood in front of her, resting his hands on her upper arms. "I'm not trying to upset you, but you need help, support, if nothing more. And the best place for that is at home. Home with your husband."

She nodded, and Dr. Laghari pulled her into a hug. "I can never replace your father, but I'm here if you need me." He wiped away a tear with his thumb and placed a kiss on top of her head.

Where was Rick? She dialed his number again. Voice-mail . . . again. He was going to be the death of her. When she saw him last, she wasn't sure he'd make it through the night. He needed help. But how do you help someone who refuses it? Maybe she should ask Adam for help. But if he found Rick before she did, he'd lock him up and throw the key into the Atlantic. Besides, she couldn't lean on Adam anymore. She had to find Rick and get through to him.

She had been researching rehabilitation facilities and found one she couldn't wait to tell him about. This one would be the very thing to get him straightened out. He would be free. He'd see and understand, then he'd have the life their parents always wanted for him.

Lord, help me help Rick. Help Adam understand that what I'm doing is for his best. Strengthen me to walk this road—alone.

Jenny lifted her head and looked around the empty sanctuary. She was alone. Well, maybe not completely alone. God was here, right?

The air shifted around her, and the church doors thudded as they bounced shut.

Jenny turned in her seat, smiled, and wagged a finger at the Kona Joe cup in Amanda's hand as she walked toward Jenny. "Should you be drinking that?"

Amanda made her way up the aisle and sat next to Jenny. "Yes. It's decaf." She took a sip and leaned back. "Joe made sure of it."

"You look good. Being pregnant looks good on you. You're glowing."

"It's sweat. Not glowing."

"Uh-huh. You're happy. And that's the glow." Jenny said as she waved her finger up and down at Amanda.

She beamed and rubbed her tummy. "I am happy." She shifted as best as she could in her seat to face Jenny. "How are you doing? I saw your car outside and I've been wanting to see you. Life's been busy, but that's no excuse."

"I'm good."

"Liar." Amanda took another sip. "Jenny, I know Ryker is Adam's closest friend. But I want you to know you can talk to me. I want to be your friend. You helped me out when I needed someone. I don't want to just return the favor, but be there for you, too."

Jenny fingered her cross. "Thank you."

"I know you still love Adam. He still loves you."

"Can I ask you a question?" Jenny asked.

"Anything?" Amanda laid her arm on the back of the pew and propped up her chin on the heel of her hand.

"How did you know your relationship was right with the Lord?"

Amanda coughed mid-sip. "Didn't see that one coming."

"I'm sorry—"

"No, it's okay." Amanda grabbed the napkin that was around her cup and wiped her chin.

"No, it's not. Never mind." Jenny sagged back in her seat and fidgeted with her phone.

"Clarify what you mean. Do you mean now? Or when I realized I needed God?"

Jenny traced the outline of her phone and shrugged. "I don't know."

Amanda ducked and tried to make eye contact with Jenny. "Hey, what's going on?"

Jenny looked at Amanda, whose face was distorted by the tears filling her eyes. "I don't know . . . I don't know what I'm doing. I don't know what I'm supposed to be doing. Everyone keeps telling me God is with me, but I never sense Him or feel Him. And now—" Jenny swiped at the tears that streamed down her cheeks.

Amanda offered Jenny a napkin. "I have plenty. I've been told pregnancy makes me messy. Joe keeps me supplied. And Ryker's taken to calling me 'Grace.'"

A quiet chuckle-hiccup-snort escaped out of Jenny.

Amanda nudged Jenny. "You should keep me around more."

"I don't know what to do, Amanda. When did you know? When did you know there was more . . . something more to this life . . . someone more?"

"We're all different. But I believe everyone experiences change. You know Ryker's story. It doesn't get more dramatic. Mine isn't like that, but when I saw him bleeding out in front of me, I knew then what I thought was important in life, wasn't. My pride kept me from so much. From everything."

"But I've been coming back to church, and I don't feel any different. I have no idea what I'm doing."

"Have you talked to Pastor Matthews?"

"Yes. But I still feel like I don't get it."

"Can I ask you a question?"

Jenny wiped her cheeks with the napkin and nodded. "Sure."

"Why are you divorcing Adam? Did he do something?"

"No."

"Did you do something that you don't want to tell him?"

"No. Not really."

"Not really?"

Jenny wrapped the napkin around her finger and dug her nail into the purple flesh at the end of her finger. She released the napkin and watched it unwind. "I guess it depends on how you look at it."

"Can you tell me?"

Jenny shook her head.

"I can't help you if you don't tell me something."

"Maybe something happened to me. Maybe God . . . maybe God," she trailed off.

Amanda scooted a little closer to Jenny and put her arm around her shoulders. "Do you remember when we were in school? Everyone thought my family was invincible. Adam hated me. But I didn't care. I had the perfect life. Cragge Automotive Group was my destiny. Ryker and I had a future planned. Then it all began to fall apart my senior year."

"I remember. And I'm sorry Adam hated you."

"Thanks. But my life wasn't perfect. And bitterness and unforgiveness ate away at me. God wasn't doing anything to help me. God didn't fix it. So, I put Him on my list," Amanda said.

"Then Ryker came back and showed you God."

"I wish. It wasn't for a lack of trying on his part. I'm pretty hardheaded. It goes with that pride thing. Anyway, when I was watching Ryker bleed in front of me, nothing mattered. I realized in that moment—all my fears, my pride, my anger—none of it mattered."

"So, then you gave your life to God?"

"I don't think so. I mean, it was the start of it, so I guess yes, but when you're sitting in a hospital waiting room waiting to find out if the man you've loved all your life is going to live, there's really only one person to turn to. I bared my soul to God that night."

"God healed Ryker."

"He did. But He didn't have to. And don't forget that mess that ripped up my family."

"How's your mom doing?"

"She's having more good days than bad now. The baby is helping too. She's so excited."

Jenny leaned her head on Amanda's shoulder. "I thought I had bared my soul to God. But He's not answering my prayers. He's not talking to me."

"Jenny, He is. But if you're looking for answers your way, you're going to miss Him."

"I don't understand."

"Are you trusting God? I mean, trusting God, no matter what? Or are you trusting God only for what you want? Are you willing to take what God has to offer because it's coming from God?"

The church doors clattered again behind them.

Goose bumps popped up on Jenny's arms, and a chill squirmed its way down to her toes. She looked behind her at a man standing at the back of the church.

Cold, hard eyes dug into her, stealing her breath. He made his way up the aisle to them, and Jenny forced air into her lungs.

"Ladies," he said with a nod. His gaze locked on Jenny, and he tilted his head. "Have we met?"

Her throat seized, and all she could do was shake her head. Ice formed in her veins, and she fought to regain her breathing.

Amanda stood and put herself between Jenny and the man in front of her.

He looked around the sanctuary.

Amanda drummed out a rapid tap on her coffee cup. "Can I help you? Are you here to see Pastor Matthews?"

He peered around Amanda and dragged his eyes over every inch of Jenny. The man stuck his hand out to Jenny. "I'm Cole, Cole Slater."

Amanda snapped her fingers and pointed to her eyes. "My eyes are up here. I asked you a question. Two, actually."

He slowly raised an eyebrow at Amanda and withdrew his hand from Jenny.

A side door opened, and Pastor Matthews' tall frame stepped into the sanctuary. "Excuse me, can I help you?"

Jenny reached up and tried to tug Amanda down, but she didn't budge.

Pastor Matthews made his way to the girls and extended his hand to Cole. "Do you have an appointment? I don't have anything on my calendar for today."

The man broke Amanda's gaze and turned. "No. I was hoping you had a gas can. I ran out of gas about a mile up the road."

Jenny rubbed her wrists and leaned back to get a better look at Cole Slater.

"I have something around here. There might even be some gas in it. It's for my lawnmower, so you won't get far."

"My bike gets good gas mileage when I let her."

"Girls, sit tight. I'll be right back." He motioned for the man to follow him and placed a firm grip on Slater's shoulder. "It's this way."

"Ladies, it was a pleasure," Slater said only to Jenny.

Those eyes . . . those cold, calculating eyes. Jenny couldn't take her eyes off his retreating form.

It couldn't be.

Seven

The basement was probably the worst place Rick should be hiding out in, but it was out of sight. He was thankful the musty room hadn't changed. And even more thankful for the old sofa that caught his fall. His head dropped back as he tried to breathe, trying to keep the pain from getting worse. Taking deep breaths without disturbing his shoulder was like cutting an onion and not crying. You can't do both.

The electricity was still on, but he couldn't risk being seen. Daylight funneled through the window wells, giving him enough light to see the holes that were still in the ceiling after all these years. His mouth twitched at the corner from the memory of darts. He and Jenny used to come down here and play darts and pool after his parents converted the basement for them. Nana would be happy to see what became of her living area.

A few less daggers pierced his shoulder. He knew he needed medical attention, but he couldn't risk it. Too much was at stake. There were only three tablets left from the acetaminophen Rick found in his parents' medicine cabinet. It wouldn't get him through the night. He needed to get more and pick up a phone. Once it got dark, he'd make his way out.

He hoisted himself off the couch and staggered up the stairs, through the kitchen and into the garage. The dim light from the kitchen windows seeped past the door. His old dirt bike sat there like it was waiting for him. He couldn't believe his parents kept it. Holding a flashlight in the hand of the arm with the bad shoulder, he searched for gasoline. Nothing. His parents' Lexus sat in the garage where it's been parked since their parents passed. Maybe he should take that instead, but that would broadcast his return and it was the last thing he needed or wanted.

Over at the storage cabinet, he found their old camping gear. He rummaged through it, looking for anything that could help him remain unseen. Backpack, sleeping bag, portable camping lantern, and first-aid kit. He tore into the kit and laughed: *Remind Mom to buy more bandages.* The yellowed, sticky note crinkled in his fingers. Maybe he should have actually given the note to his mom. The sharp pain and throbbing in his shoulder reminded him not to laugh.

A March snowstorm threatened to slam into Maine tonight or tomorrow. Forecasters were predicting it to be one of the worst ones Maine has seen in years. Rick needed to be out of the area before it hit. Today's unusually warm temps made him wish he could have gotten out earlier, but he had one more thing he needed to take care of before he could leave, in addition to numbing the pain radiating down his arm.

The kitchen door clicked into place, and Rick carried the camping gear to the basement door. He nudged the backpack and sleeping bag down the stairs with his foot and sat the portable lamp by the door. He'd grab it on his way back down.

Rick slowly made his way to his father's den. The mahogany desk sat intact. The room looked like it was waiting for his dad to come home and take his place behind the big old desk. How many times had he and his father sat in this room and discussed politics? How many times did they talk about Rick's girlfriends or his future?

The house stood still, waiting for life to pick up where it had once been. Active. Vibrant. And loving, if Rick was honest. It surprised him Jenny hadn't sold their parents' home or that she and Adam hadn't moved in.

He leaned against the bookcase, then slid down and pinched his eyes shut. Dust and grit stuck in Rick's throat. A tear flowed freely out of the corner of his eye, then sobs took over and pitched through his whole body. What he wouldn't give to go back and redo his life. He'd give anything to make his dad proud. If only his father could have passed away, knowing his son made something of himself.

But his dad was gone and never coming back. Rick didn't think he could have made things worse or his life any more of a mess.

More pain surged down Rick's arm, pulling him from that agony to an agony he'd gotten too acquainted with over the last couple of days. He pulled himself off the floor, and at the door, he knocked twice on the frame like he used to do when he was leaving his dad's den. "I'm sorry, Dad."

Light glinted off the glass in his dad's cabinet and caught Rick's eye. The gun cabinet—Dad's gun collection.

Now he was thankful Jenny hadn't sold the house or changed a thing. He owed her even more.

He went over to his dad's desk to get the key. In the center of the blotter on top of the old desk sat a legal folder from his uncle, his father's attorney. *Last Will & Testament of Dr. Alan Carver Bennett and Mrs. Teresa Marie Bennett* was embossed across the top.

"You always had to have the last word, didn't you, Dad?" Rick muttered to himself.

He ran his finger down the folder, leaving a trail through the dust. He lifted the cover and recognized his uncle's letterhead. The leather chair glided silently out from under the desk and he eased himself into it. Resting his parents' will on his lap, he turned in the chair toward the light coming in through the window.

The Atlantic Ocean rippled and cascaded off the shoreline of his parents' property. Rick loved the view from this room. He loved this house. The small rowboat was still tied to the dock. A smile drifted into a broad grin. The last time he'd been on the little boat was with Jenny. They were playing pirates and he lost when the boat flipped because she started jumping up and down in it. Her laugh. Her giggle. He was going to miss his sister.

He messed up and messed up big. Now he needed to protect Jenny. It was the least he could do.

Jenny had been after him to read the will since their parents' funeral. He still didn't want to read it, but he had questions. Maybe he'd find the answers before he left town . . . and disappeared for good.

The first page of the will was standard. Uncle Edward and Aunt Louise were executors until Jenny was of age. Nothing looked unusual for a will or for his dad. He turned the page, read it, then reread it. The page blurred, and he rubbed his eyes. "Oh, man." Now he knew why Jenny wanted him to read the will.

The house, this house, was his. He leaned back in the chair and ran a hand over the scruff he'd started sporting. He read it again . . . the house was his . . . all of it. If things could only be different.

He'd been curious why Jenny and Adam hadn't moved in here after they married, and now it made sense why she didn't treat this house like it was her house, her childhood home.

He read the rest of the will. From what he could see, Jenny hadn't touched a thing their parents left her. He wondered if that was because of Adam. Did Adam even know? Or did Adam's pride get in the way? He didn't understand Adam sometimes. He never accepted help and always acted like he had something to prove.

Rick was never going to be able to pay Jenny back for everything she'd done for him.

He turned back to face the desk and opened the drawer that still held his dad's stationery. The man hated how impersonal email was and used to send actual letters. Rick pulled out a couple of pieces of paper and a pen.

When he finished writing, he grabbed envelopes from the same drawer, wrote on them and slipped them inside the cover of his parents' will.

The throbbing in his shoulder reminded him it was time to take the last of his acetaminophen. Rick stood, placed the will back in the center of his dad's desk, and settled the chair back in place.

He grabbed the key to the gun cabinet and made quick work of it.

An original Remington 1911 gleamed in the drawer. He fondly brushed his hand over his favorite pistol, remembering when his dad taught him to shoot it. In the next drawer, he found the magazine and .45 ammo. The compact Ruger .22 revolver would be a perfect backup piece he could easily tuck away.

Rick replaced the key, and on his way out the door, turned back and gave the den one last look, scanning every inch. "I'm sorry, Dad. I messed up. I lived up to your greatest fear. But I'm going to make this right, you'll see."

After making sure the main level of the house was locked up and the guns were stashed in the garage, Rick headed back down to the basement.

Exhaustion was taking over, and he needed those last couple of pills. He still had a few hours until nightfall. A few hours to rest before he could leave town for good.

Rick flipped on the camping lantern.

"Afraid of the dark, Ricky?"

Rick's blood went cold. Out of the shadows, a man appeared.

"Slater." Rick swallowed the bile that rose in his throat.

"You're looking a little worse for wear." Slater looked around the basement. "Nice place. Did you really think you could hide? I hope you don't mind, but I gave myself a little tour. I prefer the upstairs." A slick sneer slipped into place.

"Come to finish the job?" Rick said through the burning in his throat.

"You have something Robert wants. I came to collect."

"I don't have it."

"You want to rethink that?"

Rick shrugged, then winced. He looked around the room and shook his head. "Nope. Don't have it."

"It might interest you to know that I met your sister. Pretty little thing."

"Don't you go near her. You hear me. Stay away from her," he growled as his hands closed into tight fists.

"Or what, Ricky? You don't look like you're in any position to threaten me."

"So, finish me off."

"I'm enjoying watching you suffer."

"Is that why your wife is on the run from you?"

Slater took a step forward into Rick's space. "Stay out of my business."

"I've made it my business, and I know where she is. Maybe I should say 'was,' because she's no longer there. Or is it here?" Rick took a step back and rubbed his chin like he was thinking. He locked eyes with Slater. "I know more than you realize. You underestimated me. If anything happens to me, Robert's entire organization will crumble."

"Empty threats. You would have done it by now. You have something that belongs to Robert, and I want it or I will go after your sister."

"Then you'll never find your wife."

"I don't need you to find her. She can't hide forever."

"But you do need me to find the flash drive."

"I should just kill you now and be done with it."

Drops of sweat rolled down Rick's back. He grasped his shoulder, trying to stop the throb that thumped in time with the shaking of his hand.

"Tell me why you should live? You're a worthless piece of trash, and I told Robert not to bring you on board. You've been nothing but a liability ever since." Slater spit in his face.

"Because I know where Robert's shipment is and where it's heading." Rick took another step back. "Maybe I'd be willing to cut you in."

"You are in no position to make me any offers." Slater pulled his phone out of his pocket and turned it toward Rick. The temperature in the room went up twenty degrees.

Rick lunged for Slater. Slater stepped out of the way. Rick stumbled and crashed into the side table. A grunt escaped when his shoulder slammed into it. He rolled himself onto the couch, trying to catch his breath, trying to ignore the pain that had exploded in it.

Slater crouched down in front of him, holding his phone for him to see. "She's beautiful when she sleeps, isn't she? In case you were wondering, I have more. Wanna see?" He began to flip through his pictures. "As you can see, Ricky, you underestimated me. Your sister is in my hands, and there's nothing you can do about it."

"Even if you kill me and you hurt Jenny, you'll have Adam to deal with."

"The cop? Yeah, I'm familiar with him. Pining away over the woman who doesn't want him. He's so focused on her, he'll never see me coming."

Rick reared back and headbutted Slater, throwing him off-balance. Rick stood and began to run. Slater recoiled and grabbed Rick from behind and flung him around so he was facing him. His fist connected with Rick's jaw, and he tumbled backward. Slater pinned him on the pool table and applied pressure to Rick's injured shoulder. He whimpered like a scared, caged dog.

"This is nothing compared to what I'm going to do to you. It's a little hard to move when it hurts this much, huh?" Slater increased the pressure.

Blood pooled in the corner of Rick's mouth from Slater's strike. Tears streamed down his face, landing on the felt of the pool table. He groaned and his entire body shook.

"Now, I'm not asking again. Where's the flash drive? Where's the shipment?" Slater pushed off Rick. "Try something stupid like that again and I will shoot you."

"Then you might as well shoot me because you'll never find the flash drive, and I'll never tell you where the shipment is heading."

Eight

The dock swayed with every step Adam took. The smell of saltwater tugged his memories loose and took him back to a day when he and his brothers used to go out with his dad on his lobster boat. Sometimes, he wished for that simpler time when life wasn't much more than hanging out with his dad on his boat and trying to get Jenny to notice him.

All the boats were back and tied up for the day, and his parents' car was still in the parking lot. Adam went to the office, and the squeaky door hinge announced his arrival. He walked back through the main room to his dad's office, where he found him bent over his desk, pecking away at the keyboard.

"Where's Mom?" Adam took a seat in one of the worn vinyl chairs in front of his dad's desk.

"She left with Mike and Melissa. I'm still trying to get this report filed." His dad grunted and smacked the backspace key.

"Why isn't Mom or Melissa doing it?" Adam picked up his dad's nameplate and ran his thumb over his name. The

"J" in Jerry had worn down and "Taylor" was as clear as the day he and his brothers gave it to him for his birthday one year.

"I'm helping."

Adam snickered. "Why? Don't one of them usually do that?"

"Yup. Just trying to help a little around here since I'm not out on the boat as much these days. Mike's been picking up the slack for me."

"Anything I can do?" Adam replaced the nameplate on his dad's desk and straightened it.

"I quit. Reports are stupid anyway, but thanks for the offer. If I keep trying to get this to work, my computer will be on the ocean floor before nightfall." Jerry took his glasses off and laid them on his desk. He leaned back in his chair and rested his elbows on the arms of the chair.

"Where's Dave?"

"Home, I guess. It's just me and this cranky computer. We missed you at church, Sunday."

"Yup." Adam looked at the chamber awards his dad hung behind his desk. "Is that one new?" He pointed to the last one in the row.

"New this year. So, will we see you this Sunday?"

Adam shrugged.

"What happened?"

"Nothing." Adam returned his gaze to his dad's.

"What do you mean?"

"Nothing happened."

"So, why are you not coming to church?" His dad shifted in his seat and rolled closer to his desk.

"Taking a break."

"Enough. What's really going on, Son?"

Adam stood and walked over to the twenty-year-old family portrait sitting on the messy bookcase. "Nothing. Absolutely nothing." He turned back to his dad. "I know you and Mom have faith. Ryker and Amanda found God. I see Mike and Melissa there, even Dave, most Sundays."

"Your mom has been so happy to see her sons in church."

"I don't think it's for me."

"Really, then what is for you?" Jerry planted his forearms on his desk.

"Huh?"

"Son, we've talked about this, and I'm happy to do it again and again with you. You know how important the Gospel is."

"Yup. And you're not the only one." Adam walked over to the little coiled heater to check the temperature. He could have sworn someone turned it up.

"So, do you believe?"

"Of course I do, but not like you guys." He held his hand over the coils. And they were every bit as cold as he expected, but hoped otherwise. "Jenny is back in church." Adam glanced at his dad. "And for her, I'd like to try."

"Don't do it for her. You do it for God."

"But it doesn't work for me. So why keep doing it?"

"What do you expect to happen? God isn't some genie you call on when you need something. And you certainly don't expect Him to act when and how you think He should."

"I get that. But why can't my life make more sense? Why can't I save my marriage?" Adam stood and returned to the seat he'd been sitting in.

"Now I see your problem."

"My problem?"

"You can't save your marriage."

"Thanks for the pep talk, Dad. You know, you and Ryker should start a club. You sound alike."

"Maybe you should listen."

"I've heard it, thanks." Adam leaned forward.

"Adam, you can't fix your marriage. Only God can do that. But you have to have a relationship with Him first. On His terms. Not on your terms."

"Yes, read your Bible, pray, go to Bible study. Got it." He placed his hands on his thighs and stood.

"It's not a checklist of to-do's. Nor is it something to mock."

"I have to go."

"Look, Adam, a couple of Sundays ago, Pastor Matthews preached on the stubbornness of hearts. You might want to read the passages he referred to." His dad rummaged around his desk.

"What are you doing?"

"Looking for the bulletin from that week."

"It's okay."

"No, it's not. You're not getting the severity of this . . . of your decisions." Jerry fanned through stacks of paper.

"Fine. I probably have the bulletin or I can look it up online. Maybe Jenny has it and I can get it from her. I'll read it if it will make you happy."

"No. Do it because it will make God happy. Not me, not Jenny, not even you, but God. You have to start with Him. He never promises an easy road, but He promises to be with you. Always."

Would it ever get easier coming here, knowing he didn't live here anymore? What Adam wouldn't do to get back here. The marriage his parents had was the one he wanted. But Jenny didn't seem to have the same plans.

After talking to his dad yesterday, he needed to try to talk to her again. Maybe trying to arrest her was a bad idea.

Not that he didn't already know that. This was making him nuts. She was making him nuts.

He pushed open the door and stepped in. Why didn't he knock? This is the very thing Ryker was talking about. He released a loud sigh and looked at the open door. He closed the door with a soft click. *Jenny's had months to get used to this.* He didn't want to get used to it. He wanted their life back.

There had to be a way to stop this divorce. So far, it didn't matter what he tried. It failed. He failed. But he knew he had to keep trying. He couldn't lose Jenny. This could be fixed, and their marriage could get back on track if she'd only open up to him.

"Jen, you here?" Adam said as he stood inside the front door. Her car was here, the lights were on, and breakfast still hung in the air. He barely had to crack into his detective skills to see she was here, somewhere.

"Jen, I need to talk to you."

A stack of papers on the dining room table caught his eye. He walked over to the table and a Boston General visitor's badge lay on top of a folder marked Confidential. Why was she in Boston? What was in the folder? Would she kill him if he looked? Of course she would. She shut him out from her records at the hospital. She shut him out of everything a long time ago.

He looked over his shoulder, still nothing. He hadn't heard a thing since he came into the house. Maybe she wasn't here. He didn't have to tell her he looked. Maybe it would give him the answers that he was so desperate to get. He picked up the badge and froze when he heard a scream.

Jenny's scream.

He tossed the badge down and headed back through the living room, down the hallway and reached for his gun that wasn't there. Just because he was on vacation didn't mean he shouldn't have his gun. But he'd locked up his service weapon. He needed to retrieve his personal one.

Another scream, and the sound of gushing water got louder as he walked down the hall.

"Jenny, honey, where are you?"

"Adam, I'm back here. I could use your help."

He walked into the bathroom to find Jenny standing in the tub, hands up high in front of where the showerhead used to be, shielding herself from the water gushing out of the pipe.

Adam held back a laugh and reached over and turned off the water. She was drenched. Her hair hung in strings, her T-shirt stuck to her. She was a mess. A beautiful mess and one he wasn't ready to give up on.

He held her gaze, and a chuckle escaped, then a full-blown belly laugh.

She glared at him and crossed her arms over herself.

Finally, getting himself under control, he said, "Most people undress before showering, Jen." Adam peered into the tub. "Why is the showerhead on the bottom of the tub?"

"Can you pass me a towel?"

"I don't think you have one big enough." Adam leaned in, grabbed Jenny around the legs, and tossed her over his shoulder. Even wet, she was like tossing a Raggedy Ann doll over his shoulder.

"Put me down! What are you doing?"

"Helping you dry off." Adam's grip tightened on Jenny as she squirmed. At the slider, he unlocked it and stepped out into the backyard in the warm sun.

He set Jenny down and pushed her hair back off her shoulders.

She took a step back and swayed, then took another step. Jenny narrowed her eyes and rubbed her upper arms.

"You're welcome, by the way," Adam said, holding back a laugh.

"A towel would have been fine."

"What were you trying to do back there?"

"Fix the shower. It squeaks."

Adam chuckled again.

"Shut it."

"Why didn't you ask me? I would have fixed it?"

Jenny jutted out her chin. "I can do it. I'm capable."

He studied her for a moment. "I've never thought you weren't capable, Jen. But let me help you. Please."

"Why? So you can have me arrested again?" Jenny backed up a couple of steps from Adam and looked around the backyard. A hose lay on the ground, and she walked over and picked it up. Holding the nozzle, she went to the spigot and turned it on.

"What are you doing?" Adam drew his brows in, looked around their backyard as he turned, stopping with his back to Jenny. When he turned to face her, she hit him in the center of his chest with a blast of icy water that spread and left him drenched and standing in a puddle.

Jenny let up. Now wearing a full grin, ear to ear, she said, "Should I stop?" She sent another blast his way.

Adam reached out and took a step toward her. "I wouldn't do that if I were you, Detective."

The next blast inched up. She shortened the blasts, aiming for his head. "If I don't stop, will you have me arrested again?" She released another blast.

"Please, Jen, stop!" Adam said between spurts of water. "That's actually why I'm here."

Jenny's smile drooped. "Do I have a matching warrant out like Rick now?" Her arm went slack as she watched Adam, waiting for him to answer.

He lunged for the hose, grabbed it with one hand, while the other went around Jenny's waist while he lifted the nozzle out of her hand and above her head. Their faces were so close–a few more inches and he could kiss her. But the apprehension he saw in her eyes stopped him.

Jenny's arms fell to her side, and she looked away. Adam tossed the hose and placed a finger under her chin and lifted her face until she was looking at him. He could see she needed a friend. Could he be that friend? Was that where he needed to begin? Adam pulled her into a hug. He wrapped his arms around her. It was like hugging an ironing board. She relaxed and her arms went around his waist. He placed a soft kiss on the top of her head.

She pulled back and stepped out of his embrace.

"Jenny, I'm sorry."

"No, I'm sorry, Adam. I shouldn't have let that happen."

"No, I mean, I'm sorry about the other night."

Fire flashed in Jenny's eyes. "You're sorry?"

"Yes, I overreacted."

"Ya think? If it wasn't for your captain, I would've been taken to the station and processed."

"I wouldn't have let it go that far."

"Right. I know you're mad at me, but that was a little too far."

"Maybe if you'd put me before Rick just once. I wouldn't have overreacted."

"You didn't overreact. Adam, you freaked out!"

"No, Jen, I didn't. I hit my breaking point!"

"Then let me go. Sign the papers."

Adam opened his mouth to speak, then closed it. He pulled out a patio chair and sat down.

"What are you doing?"

"Getting comfortable. Join me, won't you?" he said with a smirk. "It's not like you can go back inside; you're wetter than a drowned rat."

Jenny stood there looking at Adam. "You're not much drier."

"I'm not leaving, Jen. Oh, and by the way, I'm on vacation. So I don't need to go back to work."

"Why? Why did you take a vacation now?"

"It was better than desk duty."

Jenny snorted.

"Hey, Ryker filled me in on Cole Slater. I don't like the guy."

"You met him?"

"Yes, on my run the other day."

"He really creeps me out."

"Did something more happen?"

"No. But there's just something about him."

"Call me if he shows up again. I'll handle it."

Jenny laughed. "I was planning on calling Amanda. I think she was ready to take the guy on."

"I heard. Ryker wasn't too happy about that, either."

Adam looked around the backyard, then back at Jenny. "Jen, why are you home? I thought you were on shift today? I was surprised to see your car in the driveway when I drove by."

Jenny pulled a chair out and dropped in it. "They put me on leave."

Adam straightened. "Why? Because of the kidnapping?"

"No."

"Why?"

Jenny looked around the backyard. "I should get the trees trimmed."

"Jen, why were you put on leave?" Adam leaned forward.

Jenny pulled her hair over her shoulder and twisted it. Water puddled on the patio. "Rick."

"What happened now? Did he show up at the hospital?"

"No. This is still a small town, and they found out he was here and that I helped him. Until he's found or until we know what happened the other night, I'm on leave." She sighed and flopped back in her chair.

Adam rested his arms on his thighs. "What's it going to take for you to see Rick is bad news? He's going to ruin your life, your future?"

"He's my brother."

"And I'm your husband. What's it going to take for you to fight for me like you do him?"

"It's not like that. You don't understand."

"Then enlighten me."

"You know that ever since Mom and Dad died, Rick's had a hard time."

"Rick was spoiled, and you picked up where your parents left off."

"That's not fair. Rick needs me."

"Rick needs to grow up, and he'll never do that until you stop catering to him."

"He needs help."

"You're not helping him." Adam stood, took off his soaked shirt, walked back to the slider, and chucked his shirt at Jenny. "I'm hungry, and I need a dry shirt. I think after I find one, I'll make myself something to eat. You want anything?"

"You can't do that. You don't live here anymore." Jenny barely half protested.

"Maybe not, but it's still my house and you're still my wife." Adam's gaze traveled over Jenny. "You might want to put on some dry clothes. I'll be in the kitchen."

Later, Jenny walked into the kitchen, dressed in dry clothes, and drying her hair with a towel. Every dish was clean, even her dishes from this morning. There was a note on the breakfast bar.

Boo,

Ran to the hardware store for a few things.
I'll be back to fix the shower.
Love, A.

She picked up the note and smiled as she traced over his messy writing. She had to admit she loved having him here, and she did love him. Always had, even when he used to tease her in grade school. She put the note down and realized she had no idea what she was doing. Did God want them together? She didn't want to need Adam. She didn't want to need anyone. But maybe Dr. Laghari was right. Maybe Amanda was right.

Was she trusting God?

A knock at the door pulled her from her thoughts.

Draping the towel over the back of the barstool, Jenny walked over to the door and peeked through the peephole.

"Jenny, it's Bethany. Edward asked me to drop off some papers. The hospital told me you were home."

The last thing she wanted right now was for Adam to see Bethany there. She had to get rid of her before he came back.

Jenny whipped the door open and pasted on a smile for her friend.

"I was hoping you were going to ignore me and I could go back to work with your papers," Bethany said as she skirted past Jenny and into the living room.

"It's not too late." Jenny stood by the open door with a cheeky grin.

"Are you saying you've changed your mind?" Bethany's bohemian skirt fluttered around her legs when she turned.

"No."

"Then what are you saying?"

"Just not today." The door handle was getting slick under Jenny's grip.

"Honey, whatever is going on, you need Adam. He loves you," Bethany said as she took a step closer to Jenny.

"This is best."

"Uh-huh. Wasn't he the one who never left your side after your parents died in that horrible car accident? Your brother was nowhere to be found."

"This is different."

"Is it?"

"How's Charlie?"

"Changing the subject? Fine. My husband is fine. He comes home tomorrow."

"I'm sure you're excited."

"I haven't seen that man in too long. But that's his job."

"I thought he left two days ago?"

"Honey, we're newlyweds. You remember what it's like to be a newlywed."

Jenny took the papers from Bethany and hugged them. "Yes, I remember."

Nine

Jenny eyed the papers Bethany brought. They meant the end of her married life with Adam. They also meant a new beginning, but was it the one she wanted? She ran her hand over the file folder, then looked down the hall where Adam was fixing their shower. Maybe it was a good time for a fire, and she had the perfect kindling for it. But was it fair to him?

Their wedding portrait that hung over the fireplace told her this was the life she wanted. And she wanted it with Adam. On the mantel was a picture of Adam sitting with a little girl at the last picnic the hospital had. Jenny had taken it without him knowing. He was intently coloring the prince, and the little girl was coloring the princess, side by side. Adam had a tiara on his head because the little girl asked him to model it so she should draw it on the princess. He had forgotten to take it off.

Adam deserved what she might never be able to give him. Children.

Was it her place to make the decision for him? No matter how well intentioned she was? She picked up the papers and thumbed the edges. The breeze blew the wisps of hair off her cheeks.

Lord, give me strength to do what I need to, what is right. Make Adam understand.

When she looked around the living room, all she saw was their story. *How do I walk away from all of this?* If Adam hadn't contested the divorce, he wouldn't be here right now fixing the shower. A quiet beat filled the room as she thumped the folder against her leg. Warmth spread through her and she relaxed.

She was still mad at him for the other night. But was Adam right? Was she putting Rick before him? Was it time to let Rick stand on his own? How did she do that? How did she let him go and still love him? How did she stop worrying about Rick?

How would Adam react when she told him the truth—the reason for the divorce, the reason for going to Boston, that she was keeping her multiple sclerosis diagnosis from him? Was this something she wanted to saddle him with for the rest of his life? Was it fair of her to do that to him? Was it fair for her to make the decision for him?

These questions were on a forever repeat in her mind.

Why was she so scared to tell him? Did she trust him to stand by her during this?

Did she trust God?

Adam was going to be so upset at her for not telling him. Maybe he would be relieved when she finally told him, and he'd forget to be mad?

What a mess I've created, but it's time to get off this hamster wheel and tell Adam the truth.

"Shower's fixed." Adam walked into the living room, drying his hands on a towel.

Jenny sprang off the couch and spun on her heel, clutching the folder to her chest. "Can we talk?"

Adam's eyebrows shot up. "Jen, I've been trying to talk to you for months."

"I know." She sat the papers down on the coffee table. "And I'm sorry." She walked over to him, reached for his hand, laced her fingers through his, and tugged him over to the couch. She sat and looked up to meet his eyes. "Can we sit and talk? Please."

"Whatever is in the papers, just know I am going to contest it. I've told you before I'm not going to make divorcing me easy," Adam said as he sat next to Jenny.

"I deserve that, but you don't understand. I need to tell you something."

"I know I don't understand. You won't talk to me. You've completely shut me out."

Jenny turned to face Adam. She placed her hands on his cheeks and turned his head toward her. "You're not listening. Adam, I don't want to shut you out any longer. I'm sorry I did. It was wrong to do that."

Adam watched his wife. Through squished cheeks, he said, "So, you're actually going to tell me what this is all about? Does this have something to do with what your uncle's paralegal brought over?"

She settled her hands back onto her lap and looked at the stack of papers on the coffee table. "I don't know. I haven't looked at them yet."

"Yet?"

"I don't want to look at them. Right now, I don't care what they say."

Adam cocked his head. "So, after all this time, you're finally going to tell me what's been going on?"

"Yes."

"Why now? What changed?"

"Nothing . . . A lot . . . Maybe being abducted the other night has me thinking."

"Does this mean you're stopping the divorce?"

Jenny sat there, looking at her wedding rings as she spun them around her finger.

"You haven't changed your mind, have you?" Adam leaned back and draped his arm over the back of the couch.

"Can we start with the why? Please? Maybe you'll want the divorce after you hear the why?"

"Boo, I told you I wasn't divorcing you." He pulled Jenny into a hug. "I love you, and you're not getting rid of me that easily. It's a promise I intend to keep."

"You can't wait forever," Jenny said into his chest, listening to the soothing rhythm of his heartbeat.

"Will you tell me what's going on?" he rumbled in her ear.

Jenny sucked in a deep, long breath, then let it out and pushed away from Adam. "I saw Dr. Laghari the other day."

"Your dad's friend?" Adam claimed Jenny's hand and tucked a strand of hair behind her ear. "What's going on, Jen? I saw the hospital badge on the table."

"I saw Dr. Laghari . . ." Her voice wavered. She took another deep breath to steady it. "I saw Dr. Laghari—"

A knock on the front door stopped Jenny and drew her attention. She let out a frustrated huff and pushed off the couch.

Adam pulled her back down. "Let it go. I've been waiting for months to have this conversation. Whoever it is will go away."

Jenny tightened her grip on Adam's hand. "Adam, I'm—"

Another knock. "Jenny, it's Ryker. I know you and Adam are in there. I need to talk to you."

Adam stood. "I'll get rid of him," he said as he stormed to the front door.

He flung open the door. "What do you want?"

"It's good to see you, too. Can we come in?" Ryker asked as he tried to push his way into the house.

"No." Adam put his hand on Ryker's chest and shoved him back out the door. "Call first next time," he said as he began to close the door.

"Wait. We had a development." Ryker wedged his booted foot in the door, preventing it from closing.

"I'm off the case and on vacation, remember? Now, please remove your foot."

"It's about Jenny's parents' house."

Jenny ran up beside Adam. "What about their house?" she said as she tugged the door open.

"Can we come in, please?"

Adam's loud grunt revealed his annoyance. "Make it quick. We were in the middle of something."

Ryker and Drew stepped through the door. Ryker closed it as he said, "Jenny, when was the last time you were at your parents' house?"

"I check on it periodically. And I've been keeping it maintained with the same people my parents used. Even their cars. But I haven't been there in a while. Why?"

"The neighbors called in a report saying they heard what they thought were gunshots."

Jenny turned and grabbed her keys and purse off the side table and headed for the door.

"What do you think you're doing?" Adam asked.

"Going to my parents' place." Her keys slipped from her grip and she bent to pick them up.

"You can't," Ryker said.

"What do you mean, 'I can't'? I most certainly can." Jenny walked around Adam.

Ryker moved in front of the door. "It's a crime scene. I can't let you go there."

Jenny took a step back. Her steps faltered. Adam reached out and grabbed her. "Come sit, Jen." He guided her to sit on the couch next to him. He took her keys and purse and laid them on the coffee table, then tucked her in next to him.

"What happened at Jenny's parents' house? Why is it a crime scene?"

Drew spoke. "It looks like someone's been staying there."

Adam closed his eyes and pinched the bridge of his nose. "Rick. Why didn't I think of that? It's where he'd be out of sight."

Jenny looked up at him. "You? I should have thought of it."

"We don't know for sure that it was Rick. When uniforms checked it out, the house was unlocked, the security alarm wasn't set, and they found blood—a lot of blood," Drew said.

"What do you mean, 'a lot of blood'?" Jenny asked.

Ryker pulled out his phone and pulled up the text from the officer on the scene. He opened the attached pictures and turned his phone toward Jenny. "Do you recognize any of these?"

She took Ryker's phone and scrolled through the rest of the pictures. She peered up at Adam. "These are Rick's things." As she continued to work her way through the pictures, she asked, "What happened? The last time I was there, the basement didn't look like this." Jenny bent closer to the phone. "Is that blood on the pool table? And why is the place such a mess? Where's Rick?" She gave Ryker his phone back.

"We need to find him," Drew said.

Ryker sat on the edge of the coffee table and scooted closer to Jenny. "Jenny, the house has an alarm. Didn't the service company call you?"

"I'm not using the service right now. This is Otter Bay. I figured if something happened, a neighbor would call the police. They know no one is living there." She stood, stepped over Ryker's legs, and started pacing.

"So, the alarm is dismantled? What about the house siren? That should work without service," Drew asked.

She stopped pacing and pivoted toward Drew. "I'm sorry. I didn't think it was necessary to keep it activated. I never set the alarm." She reached around Ryker and grabbed her things. "I want to see the house. I have to go."

Adam stood and stepped into her path. "No, Jen, you can't go."

"Why not? Someone has to clean it up; someone has to find Rick. I can do those things." Jenny fumbled with her keys and took a step back.

"You can find Rick?" Adam took Jenny's hands in his. "You know you can't find him. Clearly, he's not there."

"But all that blood. How could he have gotten out of there?" She gasped and pulled out of Adam's grip. "I have to go. What if someone took him? What if they took him like they did me?" Her voice cracked.

"Jenny, breathe. Honey, you're not doing yourself any good." Adam pulled her back and wrapped his arms around her.

"Ryker, when can I get in there?"

"You can't. I'm sorry, Jenny," Ryker said.

"She can't, but I can." Adam turned to Jenny. "You stay here. I'll let you know what's going on and if I see Rick." He pulled his keys out of his pocket. "I just need to make a quick stop on the way."

"You're on vacation, remember?" Ryker chided him.

"Jenny, I'll be back, and then we'll finish our conversation."

"Why can't I go with you? It's my family's home."

"Please Jenny, wait here for me. Let me check it out first. Wait for me, please."

"Adam—" Jenny began, but Adam stopped her with a kiss.

"Stay here. I'll be back, I promise. Will you wait for me?"

Jenny closed her eyes and bit her lower lip.

"Please, Jen. Be here when I get back. Promise me."

Ten

Adam parked his SUV behind the cruiser that sat in front of Jenny's parents' house. Crime scene tape stretched across the front door. He signed the crime scene entry log, ducked under the tape, and walked into the living room. Ryker and Drew had their heads together in the middle of the room.

The room was immaculate. Not even a speck of dust dared to be seen in this room. He walked over to Ryker and Drew. "Everything seems to be fine here."

"The party's downstairs." Ryker walked to the basement door and disappeared down the stairs. Adam and Drew followed.

At the bottom of the stairs, Adam let out a low, slow whistle. "Quite the party." A busted lamp, turned-over end table, couch cushions scattered, and blood everywhere he looked. The pool table looked like someone bled out on it.

Drew handed Adam a pair of gloves.

"Do you recognize anything?" Ryker asked.

Bloody towels piled on the floor in front of the fireplace. A torn shirt. Blankets and a pillow tossed into a pile. Adam toed the pile and glanced over at Ryker and Drew. "Was Rick's room searched?"

Drew stepped away from the pool table. "Uniforms cleared the house when they arrived on the scene. No one is here. We're just getting started on combing this place. Do you know how long it's been since Jenny or Rick have been here?"

Adam used his shoulder to rub the perspiration off the underside of his jaw, and he fanned himself with his jacket. "Why is it so hot in here?"

"The only thing we can figure is Rick thought it would be safe to run the heat in the daylight. Maybe he figured neighbors would think it was Jenny who was here or that they wouldn't see the furnace running," Drew replied.

"Let's get that thing turned down. He must be running one heck of a fever. We need to find him before the infection kills him. If he's not already dead somewhere." Adam picked his way around the basement again. "It looks like Rick kept to this area. But who else was down here with him? This is a lot of blood." Adam continued through the basement. He let out a frustrated sigh and closed his eyes. "I'm going to kill him when I find him. What was he thinking, bringing this here? What if Jenny had come by?"

"When was the last time you knew of either of them having come by here?" Ryker asked.

"I don't know. You'd have to ask Jenny. You heard her. She checks on the place periodically, and as far as I know, when she saw Rick the other day, it was the first time in a long time."

"Does she check the entire house when she's here?"

"I don't know." Adam looked around the room again. "Where did he go? With all this blood loss, where is he? From the look and lack of a rotten odor, it hasn't been that long since he was here."

"Uniforms have started canvassing. Nightfall isn't too far off. We need to find him," Drew said.

"Right, it's still daylight. How far could someone in this condition get without someone seeing something?" Adam said.

Adam pulled out his cell phone, scrolled through his contacts, and pressed Rick's number. "Rick, call me. I'm at the house."

"You know he won't answer your call," Ryker said.

"I have to try." Adam hit another key on his phone. "Hey, Jen. Have you heard from Rick?" Adam nodded once and massaged his forehead as he paced. "If you do, call me immediately." He pinched the bridge of his nose. "Please . . . Okay. And don't leave the house without letting me know. With your parents' house being a crime scene, it's not safe. Promise me, Jen . . . Keep the house locked up. See you soon." Adam hung up and stowed his phone. "She thinks he lost his phone. She's been trying to reach him for days. I want to see upstairs."

Adam headed to the stairs as Captain Danvers emerged from the stairwell.

"Detective Taylor. I thought you were on vacation."

"I am, sir. Just came at Ryker and Drew's request to help with the scene."

"Make sure that's all you do." The captain turned toward Ryker and Drew. "What do you know?"

Ryker's voice faded into the background as Adam slipped upstairs.

Adam stood in the living room. Everything was pristine. On the mantel was a picture of him and Jenny on their wedding day. With his hand still gloved, he picked up the picture.

"Oh, Jenny, I wish I knew what was going on." Jenny's smile was effortless and reached from ear to ear. They were so happy.

Her parents were still with them, and Adam's big family filled the place. It turned into the party of the century. No two families got along better.

He squeezed his eyes shut, trying to imagine his life without Jenny in it. Anytime he pictured his future, she was there, with him every step of the way. When he opened his eyes, there she was, smiling, like she was telling him it was the happiest day in her life.

Leave it to Rick to mess it up for us when she was about to tell me what was going on.

With a deep, weary sigh, he replaced the picture.

It was time to get home to his wife, but first he wanted to look around. Rick couldn't have gotten far.

Adam stepped into the den and stopped at the gun cabinet. Two empty dust-free spaces stared at him where pistols once lay. The Remington was gone, and a .22 was not where it should be. Adam carefully pulled each drawer open. The magazine for the Remington was gone, too, as he expected.

He walked over to the desk, and nothing was out of place. Jenny and Rick's parents' will lay in the center of the desktop.

Before he went to find Ryker and Drew to tell them about the missing guns, Adam headed to Rick's room. He passed the hall bathroom and stopped to speak with Myers. "Have you guys found anything yet?"

"Nope. Aside from the basement, clean as a whistle."

"Has anyone checked Rick's room or his parents'?"

"Not yet."

"Okay, I'm going to have a look in Rick's room. Maybe I'll see something."

The officer resumed his search of the cabinets as Adam headed to Rick's bedroom.

The room was bigger than he remembered. He did a three-sixty around the room. Not wanting to break protocol . . . too much, he wanted to be the one to search it. Rick's bed hadn't been slept in, and none of the linens were disturbed. The closet door was ajar. Adam walked over and flipped on the light, then stepped into the closet. Nothing looked out of place. Rick's clothes hung straight on hangers, arranged by color. Shoes lined the bottom; sweaters, sweatshirts, and shoeboxes neatly lined the shelves. Adam never realized Rick had a particular side to him. He pushed the clothes toward the back of the closet, revealing nothing but a clean wall, not even a scuff.

Adam found Ryker, Drew, and Captain Danvers in the living room.

"I thought you left." Danvers tapped his belt with his finger.

"I found something," Adam replied.

"Detective, will suspending you get you to stay out of the investigation?"

Adam regarded his captain, warring with just how much truth was safe to say to him.

"No, sir. You don't have to suspend me."

"Good."

"But before I go, I'd like to show you something. Something that if you didn't know Jenny and Rick's father, you might miss."

"Fine. But after this, you're done. Do you understand?"

"Yes, sir."

The men made their way back to the den. Adam showed them the gun cabinet with the missing guns. "There should be a Remington 1911 in here and a .22 revolver is missing."

"You sure?"

"Yes, sir."

"Whoever took it didn't mess around. The Remington is not something for a novice," Captain Danvers said.

"It might explain all the blood downstairs." Ryker peered into the case.

"Were any shell casings found in the basement?" the captain asked.

"Not a one," Drew answered.

"Anything else out of place?" Captain Danvers pulled out the drawers to the gun cabinet.

"Nothing else that I've seen, sir."

"Let's have it dusted for prints. Maybe something will turn up," Captain Danvers said. "As far as you know, when Rick was at your house, he was alone?"

"From what I know, yes. But you'd have to ask Jenny. I think he was running from someone." Adam looked around the room. "Like maybe the person who shot him."

"And he caught up with him."

"Then where did they go?" Ryker asked.

"The million-dollar question," Drew replied.

Adam turned toward the window. The small boat tied to the dock rode the current like any other day.

His phone rang. "Hey, Dad."

Adam turned away from the window and felt the color drain from his face. "Where is he? Is he going to be okay?" He ran his hand through his hair and rubbed the back of his neck. "I'm on the way."

Adam looked between Ryker and Captain Danvers. "Mike's been stabbed. I gotta go."

Eleven

The papers on Jenny's lap were exactly what she had asked for. If only she hadn't answered the door, then Bethany could have taken them back to the office. It was the next phase—after the divorce was final.

The divorce. Maybe getting interrupted was a good thing. Except now, she really wanted to talk to Adam and tell him everything.

She chucked the papers to the other end of the couch. The pins and needles tingled again in her fingers and she wiggled them, trying to get the feeling back. Maybe it was time to move up the next doctor's appointment. This was happening too much.

No, she wasn't thinking. She should be thanking Ryker for interrupting her. Adam didn't need to be saddled with her or her disease. He deserved the life she couldn't give him.

Everything was a mess! A missing brother, her parents gone, and an illness that now controlled her life. And somewhere in this mess, she was supposed to believe God was with her. *Right.*

Jenny leaned back into the corner of the couch, punched the couch pillow, and snuggled in. An afghan that Adam's mother made them was draped over the back of the sofa. She grabbed it and covered herself, then she pulled it over her head and wept.

A knock on the door startled her. She jumped and tangled herself up in the blanket—falling and tripping, some of the papers from her uncle scattering to the floor.

Dragging the blanket with her, another rap on the door had her fumbling to get it.

She flung the door open, and the blanket fell to the ground.

"Rick!"

Jenny's body chilled without the blanket, and she was grateful she had the door to hold her up as disappointment filled her. "Hi, can I help you?"

"Jenny, right?"

Jenny looked at the woman, and then recognition brightened her face. "Mary, right? Amanda and Ryker's housekeeper?"

Nervously, the woman looked over her shoulder and down the street, then up the other side. "May I come in?"

"Is Amanda okay?" Jenny stepped back and picked up the blanket as Mary entered. Jenny stuck her head out the door and looked up and down the street.

Mary's eyebrows drew in. "Huh? Oh, she's fine. That's not why I'm here. I'm actually looking for Rick."

"Rick? My brother, Rick? How do you know him?" Jenny closed the door and rolled the blanket around her arms like a giant muff.

"He helped me out. I need to get in touch with him." Mary looked around the house and fixated on the pictures over the fireplace.

"Get in line. I haven't been able to get ahold of him in a while myself."

Jenny shook the blanket out, folded it, and chucked it over to the couch. More papers fluttered in the air when it landed. She propped a knee on the arm of the couch and kept her eyes glued to the woman in front of her. "How long have you lived in Otter Bay?"

"Not long," Mary said to the mantel.

"Because Rick sent you?"

Mary turned around. "He spoke highly of Otter Bay, and the way he talked about it, I had to see it for myself."

"Why are you looking for Rick?" Jenny took a step closer to Mary and crossed her arms. "How did you know he was in Otter Bay? I didn't know until the other night."

"I told you, we're friends." Mary gave Jenny a nervous half smile.

"Are you the reason he was shot?"

"What! Rick was shot? I have to go." Mary took a step toward the door.

"Wait a minute." Jenny held up a hand, halting Mary's progress. "Tell me what's going on."

"I can't. I promised. Please, I have to go."

"Promised who? Rick?"

"Yes, Rick, of course." Mary's words disappeared into the air.

The house phone rang. "Maybe that's Rick now." She prayed it was him because he was going to get a piece of her mind.

Jenny snatched the phone off the wall in the kitchen, but before she could even say hello—"I just got a call from a kid on the dock and they're taking Mike to the ER." The anguish in Adam's mother's voice made Jenny clutch the countertop for support.

"Wait. What?! What happened?" Jenny climbed onto one of the barstools at the breakfast bar. A corner of Adam's note was still tucked under a coaster. As she listened to Adam's mother, she traced Adam's note and straightened out the bent corner.

"He got into a fight with someone," she said through tears.

"Has Adam been called?"

"Dad called him. He's on the way. I thought you might want to come in. It's bad, Jenny," Adam's mother said as she sobbed into the phone.

Jenny's cell phone started ringing from the living room. "I'll be there."

Jenny turned, slipped off the barstool, and grabbed her cell phone.

The front door was open. Mary was gone.

She grabbed her phone off the end table and answered it. "I'm on my way." The hospital was a short distance away.

After a quick change into her scrubs, she set the alarm, locked up, and was out the door.

Adam barreled through the ER doors and slid to a stop at the nurses' station. The muscles between his shoulders pulled taut. He leaned over the counter and scanned the nurses' work area. His dad came up behind him and rested his hand on his shoulder. "Son, there's no news yet."

"What happened?" Adam spun and faced his father.

"Adam." His mom cried and wrapped her arms around him.

Adam returned the hug. He closed his eyes, rested his cheek on the top of her head, and drew her in a little closer.

"Glad you could make it." Melissa's chin quivered, and she fidgeted with a tissue in her hand. Pieces of it fell to the floor.

Adam released his mom and pulled Melissa into a tight hug. "Mel, Mike's going to be okay. You'll see."

"He was doing so well. I don't understand. We were reconciling. He had just moved back home. We were a family again, Adam. I don't understand." Melissa cried into his shirt.

"What happened?" Adam said to his father over Melissa's head.

"Son, sit down."

"Tell me what happened."

His dad scrubbed his rough, calloused hands down his face. "There was a fight at the dock. After work. He wasn't supposed to be there."

"He's been doing so good, too," his mother said through her tears.

Adam watched his mom crumple in his dad's arms.

The outside ER doors swung open, and the last of the Taylor clan bolted through.

"Dave, over here," Dad hollered.

"What's going on? Why was Mike at the dock after we closed up? And why was he left alone?" Dave's tone could cut steel.

"Mike was knifed. It's bad," Adam's mother said from the security of her husband's arms.

"The kid who called your mom said Mike got into it with his drug dealer. We're not sure if he was trying to buy drugs or if he was trying to pay the guy off or if he . . . or . . . we don't know."

Adam looked around the waiting room, then over to the nurses' station.

"I called Jenny." Adam's mom sniffed. "She said she'd be here, but she hasn't shown up yet."

They began to head into the waiting room when the doors leading to the patient area opened, and Jenny came out, followed by an ER doctor.

"Jerry and Janet Taylor, I'm Dr. Edwards."

"How's my baby?" Adam's mother reached for Melissa.

"When can I see my husband?" Melissa latched on to Janet.

"How bad is it?" Adam's father asked.

Jenny's sad eyes locked on Adam's. It was the same look she gave him when she didn't want to tell him something that would upset him.

"Excuse me, I'm his wife." Melissa stepped closer to Adam's mom.

"We're working on keeping him stabilized. Then we can operate. We don't know the extent of his injuries. He's lost a lot of blood."

"How long until you can operate?" Dave asked.

Adam watched Jenny spin her wedding ring around her finger and flex all of them. What he wouldn't give to have her in his arms right now, too.

Dr. Edwards looked at Melissa. "His wounds are extensive. I need to get back. As soon as we can move him, we'll let you know."

Dr. Edwards slipped back through the door and disappeared.

Adam's mom clutched on to Melissa, and they cried. Adam's dad wrapped his arms around them both.

Dave turned to Jenny. "Be straight with us. He's going to make it, right?"

"I'm praying. He's lost a lot of blood, Dave. Everyone is doing the best they can. I promise."

Jenny reached out and grabbed Adam's hand, which closed around hers, and he took a step closer.

"Adam, we're doing everything we can. As soon as your mom called, I came right over. The hospital lifted my leave so I could be with him."

"Thank you, dear," Adam's mom said.

Jenny gave Adam's hand a squeeze. "I've got to get back there. I promise I'll be back, and as soon as you can see him, I'll come get you."

Adam stood and crushed the paper cup. He walked over to the window and watched cars cruise up and down the main road.

His mom came up behind and rubbed his back. She leaned her head on his arm. Adam reached around and hugged her.

"He'll be okay. He has to be," she said.

"I hope so, Mom. I hope so."

"Jenny looked good. A little thin, but good. How are you two doing?"

Adam shrugged. "Same, I guess."

"Don't give up. You have to have faith."

"I hope your faith works its magic for Mike."

"You know what I mean."

"Mom, this faith thing may work for you and Dad, and it may work for Ryker and Amanda, but it's never worked for me and Jenny."

"You don't know that." Janet tightened her hug

"Yes, I do. She hasn't stopped the divorce."

"Son, don't let her go."

"She was finally ready to tell me why, then we got interrupted. I don't get the feeling she's ready to give up the idea of a divorce."

Dave walked up and stood looking out the window. "Are they looking for the guy who stabbed Mike?"

"I just got off the phone with Ryker a few minutes ago. They're looking for him." Adam released his mom from the hug.

"What about the guy who called Mom?" Dave said to the window.

"They're looking for him, too," Adam spoke to Dave's reflection.

"I can't believe Mike would throw away all his hard work! Something more was going on. He wouldn't have done this. I don't believe for a minute he was using again."

"He wasn't," Melissa said from behind them. "I would have known. A wife always does."

"Did he owe the guy money?" Adam asked.

"I don't think so. But why else would he have met with him?" Melissa answered.

The bang of the hospital doors had them all turning. Dr. Edwards and Jenny headed their way.

Jenny's head was down, her hands clenched so tight her knuckles were white.

Adam's heart spiraled; his words caught in his throat.

Jenny looked up and met his eyes. Adam was greeted with red, swollen eyes and tearstained cheeks.

She gave him a slight shake of her head.

"Mr. and Mrs. Taylor, Melissa. I'm sorry. Mike didn't make it," Dr. Edwards said.

"What? No. You're wrong. He couldn't be . . . He can't be . . . We have our entire future ahead of us." Melissa's face drained of all color. "Jenny, tell me he's wrong."

"I'm sorry, so so sorry. We did everything we could." Jenny wiped a tear away.

"No, Jenny, there has to be more you can do," Melissa begged.

"My baby is gone. He's gone." Adam's mom's knees gave out. Before she could collapse to the floor, his dad pulled her up into his arms.

"I thought you were stabilizing him." Shock and disbelief laced Dave's words.

"He lost too much blood. I'm sorry," Dr. Edwards said. "When he coded, we couldn't bring him back. I'm so sorry."

"Sorry isn't good enough!" Dave yelled.

Adam watched Jenny flinch at Dave's words, and it snapped him back to the present. His heart physically hurt in his chest. He rubbed his chest, trying to loosen the tightness. Everything around him faded, and all he could see was the last time he saw Mike. Mike had shown up at his parents' house with his six-month sobriety chip. It was just last week. He was never prouder of him.

This was wrong, very wrong.

Adam turned his gaze back to Jenny.

"Adam, you have to catch these guys. Mike is owed that," Dave demanded.

"Don't you think I know that?" Every frustration Adam had with Mike's drug abuse and the rise of drugs in Otter Bay mocked him. He failed Mike. He failed his family.

He failed—again!

"You should have already caught them. You have to know who they are. Why haven't you arrested them already? Are you happy now?" Dave moved into Adam's space.

"You're blaming me now? This is my fault?"

"Yeah, from where I'm standing, I think it is." Dave was now toe to toe with Adam.

"Dave! Knock it off. We don't need this right now, Son," their dad warned.

"I think it's about time for Adam to man up. He was always too good for us. He was too good for the family business. What was it he said? Oh, right, lobsters aren't in his blood." Dave glared. "But they were good enough to put a roof over his head."

"Son, stop! Before you say something you can't take back."

"I don't want to take it back. Adam had to be the big crime fighter, but he couldn't even protect his little brother. Make a difference, he said. His own wife doesn't even want anything to do with him."

"That's enough!" their father roared.

Melissa turned her attention to Dr. Edwards. "Can I . . . Can I . . ." She tried to take another breath. Strong arms surrounded her–Dad.

"Can she say goodbye?" Dad spoke for her.

"Of course. We're cleaning him up now. As soon as you can see him, we'll come get you," Dr. Edwards said, then left the waiting area.

Dave shoved Adam's shoulder. "How about it, Superman? Maybe murder is enough to bring in a drug dealer since you left him free on the streets."

"This is not his fault!" Janet cried.

"Dave, please," Jenny soothed.

"Maybe Dave's right." Adam stepped back. "I couldn't protect my brother, and I can't seem to hold on to my wife."

"Don't listen to him," his dad said. "He's hurting. We all are."

"Please," Jenny pleaded.

Dave stepped into Adam's space again. "What's it going to take for you to man up? It's not hard to figure out why Jenny is divorcing you."

Dave stumbled backward when Adam shoved him hard with both hands. He recovered and lunged for Adam, grabbing him around the waist, sending them both to the floor.

Adam locked his legs around his brother's back and blocked a punch. He flipped him over so Dave was now on the floor. "You're nothing but a bully. You always have been. As soon as something gets hard, all you want to do is tear people down. Does it make you feel better?"

Breathless, Dave said, "At least I do something."

Adam shoved off the ground and stormed out of the hospital.

"Adam, wait!" Jenny shouted, and took off after him. "Adam, please. Don't leave," Jenny cried as she ran up to his SUV. "You can't leave like this."

"He's right, you know." Adam yanked the door to his SUV open.

"No, he's not." She came around the door and placed her hand on his arm. "You're a good man, Adam Taylor."

"But not good enough for you, right, Jen?"

"Please. You don't understand."

"Am I too stupid, or you don't trust me? Or you just no longer love me?" Adam slammed the door closed and leaned against it with his arms crossed. He could feel the color drain from his face. "That's it, isn't it? You no longer love me."

"No, that's not true." Jenny tugged his forearms, but they wouldn't budge.

"I don't think you have the guts to tell me the truth. Dave was right."

"No, he's not."

"You want a divorce? Fine. You got it. Now maybe I can say I've made someone happy."

"I do love you."

"Right. If you loved me, you wouldn't shut me out of your life. We're supposed to be here for each other and share our lives. Together." Adam took a deep breath and looked back at the hospital. "No, Dave was right. I'm a failure. You've shut me out, and I couldn't help Mike. I should have done more. I shouldn't have given up." He opened his door again and stepped behind it.

"You didn't give up."

"I should have done more." The tightness in his chest suffocated him a little more with each breath. "You win, Jen. The divorce is all yours." Adam buckled himself into his SUV and started it.

"Please, Adam, wait."

"For what? Did you change your mind about the divorce? Have you suddenly decided I'm worthy of your commitment and love?"

Jenny stepped closer. "Adam—"

"I don't understand. Right. I know." He put the vehicle in reverse.

"Please."

He nodded and backed out of the parking space, leaving Jenny to watch his SUV disappear out of the hospital's lot.

Twelve

Two a.m. and another sleepless night. Insomnia filled Jenny's nights more than sleep. The depression was mounting. Something had to give. Maybe a fresh start in Boston would help.

But was Adam right earlier? No, she loved him, and she trusted him with her life. But she didn't want his pity, and she didn't want him wondering if he made a mistake by sticking it out with her.

She walked over to the dining room table and picked up her Boston General visitor's badge. Is this really what she wanted? She blew out a breath and chucked it across the table.

Walking around the house had become a nightly routine. When she made her rounds into the living room, she sat on the arm of the couch and leaned back. Every night she talked to the pictures on the mantel. They made her happy when she closed her eyes and revisited the memories. These pictures meant so much to her, and they reminded her of when she had a future with Adam and her

139

family. Before it was all ripped from her. Such happy times in her life, in their lives.

Like the other nights, she went over to the picture of her parents from her and Adam's wedding and picked it up. "I miss you. I miss you both so much, it hurts." The pewter frame was cool against her skin. "I don't know what to do."

The recliner caught her as she dropped into it and curled up. She laid the picture on her lap and traced her parents' smiling faces. Tears splashed on the frame's glass. The room blurred when she looked up at the ceiling. She grabbed a tissue off the table next to her and dried her tears, then took in the room.

Alone. She was alone, and it was probably the way she would spend the rest of her life. Her life looked nothing like the life her parents had and as they smiled up at her from her lap, she said, "I miss you. And I'm tired. I'm tired of crying all the time. I'm tired of second-guessing myself. I'm tired of doing this alone. And I'm tired of being sick." Jenny dabbed her tears. She rubbed her eyes until she saw stars. A deep yawn that filled every bone in her body took over. She stood and returned the picture to its place on the mantel. "I love you."

Jenny headed toward the kitchen, and last week's church bulletin lay on top of her Bible by the couch. The Scripture on the front caught her eye. *"We urge you, brethren, admonish the unruly, encourage the fainthearted, help the weak, be patient with everyone.*" 1 Thessalonians 5:14. She had underlined 'help the weak and be patient with everyone.'

She was the weak and felt it. But who was she letting help her? Was she giving anyone the chance to help her? Was she being patient with others? Or was she just going through the motions? Was she pretending? And if she was pretending, did she have any right to question God?

Jenny glanced back at her parents' picture. Their faith was rock solid. It's what she wanted.

Another yawn snuck up on her. Exhaustion was finally going to settle in so she could get some sleep. One last look at the bulletin, and she made a mental note to call Pastor Matthews. Maybe she'd call Amanda; she believed she could trust her.

She stopped in the kitchen and filled a glass with water, guzzled it and reached to set it on the counter, when the glass slipped from her grip and shattered on the tile floor. Shards of glass scattered in all directions. A shaky hand flew to her chest. "Great! Just what I needed at this hour." Jenny stared at the broken glass. "What a mess. Just like what I'm doing now to my life."

Maybe it was time to stop waiting on people to do what she expected. Maybe it was time to make things right . . . and let God do the rest.

She picked up her phone and pulled up Adam's number, then looked at the clock. She hadn't heard from him since he'd pulled out of the hospital's parking lot, and she'd left him several messages.

The glow from her phone bounced off the broken pieces of glass on her floor. Setting her phone down, she tiptoed over the broken shards and grabbed the broom and dustpan from the laundry room.

She dumped the last few pieces of broken glass in the trash can when she heard a thud against her front door. Jenny froze. Her heart seized in her throat.

The doorknob rattled.

Adam?

Jenny tiptoed over to the door and looked through the peephole. She jerked open the door and hissed, "Get in here! Where have you been? All of Otter Bay is looking for you." Jenny reached out and grabbed Rick by the arm and yanked him inside, then slammed and locked the door.

Rick stumbled into the living room and flopped onto her couch. "I need to get out of town."

Jenny stood there for a minute with her hands fisted at her sides. Adrenaline ignited a fire that started in her belly and woke every cell in her body. She marched over and pulled back Rick's jacket, exposing his shoulder. "Looks like the bleeding stopped."

"Barely." Rick said it like it was the only thing he had energy for.

"Whose blood is all over the basement, Rick?" Jenny stood and leaned over him, trying to make herself look bigger.

"You saw that." Rick shifted on the couch. "Wait, what did you find in the house?" He coughed, clearing his throat.

"The police found lots and lots of blood. What'd you think? I'd never find out?"

"Not yet, no. Is that all?" He scooted back a little farther and looked up at Jenny, then slid back a little more.

"What's going on?" Jenny leaned closer to Rick. "You're not bleeding enough. Whose blood is that, Rick?"

"I need your car."

Jenny stepped away from her brother and grabbed her phone from the kitchen, and punched in a text message.

"Please don't call Adam." Rick looked around the room. "Where are your keys?"

"So, whose blood is all over the basement?" She tapped her palm with her phone, impatiently waiting for Rick to answer her.

"Don't worry about it, okay?" He moved into more of a sitting position and laid his head against the back of the couch, and his eyes drifted closed.

"No, not okay. I'm done making excuses for you, Rick. You need help and not the kind I can give you."

"Please, Jen."

"And who's Mary? Why did you tell her about Otter Bay and Amanda and Ryker?"

Rick straightened up and looked at her.

"She was here, Rick. Looking for you." Jenny pointed at Rick with her phone. "That's right. You. Looking for you."

"Jen, please, your car. My letters will explain everything. You'll understand then."

She spun on her heel and went over to the recliner and sat down, shifted back and tucked in, and smiled. "Enlighten me now, dear brother. What letters?"

"Jen, please. I really don't have time for this. Whatever you want, I'll do it. I need your car. You'll be safer."

"You'll do anything? Then tell me what's going on. What's really going on."

Rick moved himself to the edge of the couch, wincing as he did.

Jenny's mouth dropped open, and she sprang to her feet. "Does this have to do with Cole Slater?"

Fear crossed Rick's face, and she saw the pieces fall into place. "It does, doesn't it? Did you bring that man here?"

"How do you know him? When? When did you meet him, Jen? He's dangerous. Stay away from him."

"It seems we've all made his acquaintance in one way or another. You're the reason he's here, aren't you? You're the reason he abducted me, aren't you?"

"He abducted you? When?" Rick jumped up off the couch and grimaced, readjusting his jacket.

"You may not need to worry about him coming after you because I may take care of you myself." Jenny stared at her brother, wondering how he got to where he was today. And that's when Adam's constant words taunted her. He was right; she couldn't fix Rick. It tore her heart apart. But he had to do it himself, not her. "What's going on, Rick? Why is there all that blood at the house? Clearly you've been staying there. What happened there? Who else was there?"

Rick held out his hand. "Keys, Jen."

"What?"

"Keys."

"No." She crossed her arms over her chest.

"What?" Rick's eyes widened in surprise and disbelief.

"I said no. N-O. It spells no." Jenny stepped closer to him.

"Fine. I can't stay here. I'll figure something else out." Rick lumbered past Jenny.

A pounding on the door stopped them both.

"Jenny, it's Ryker."

Jenny shoved past Rick, then turned back and shook her finger in her brother's face. "Don't move. I mean it. I may be in possession of some of Adam's guns, and I may not be afraid to use one myself."

Jenny unlocked the door and swung it open wide, letting in the cold air.

Ryker entered and went straight for Rick. "Richard Bennett, you are under arrest."

"Why did you do this, Jenny?" Rick stepped back toward the couch.

"You need to learn for yourself. I can't keep bailing you out. Adam's right. I'm not helping you. It's only making things worse." Jenny closed the door and turned back to Ryker and Rick.

Rick planted himself back on the couch and refused eye contact with Ryker. "I'm not going."

"Have you talked to Adam? I've been trying to reach him," Jenny asked as she walked over and rested a hip against the back of the couch.

"I know. He's hurting, Jen. Give him some time."

"Is he okay?" Jenny played with the afghan fringe hanging over the couch.

"As good as he can be."

Jenny nodded toward her brother. "He's going to need medical attention."

"I'll get him looked at. Come on, Bennett."

"No," Rick said, still refusing eye contact.

"No? You don't tell your arresting officer no. And as a family friend, don't be stupid."

"As a family friend, I can't go to jail. Not yet."

"By the way," Jenny started, "did you know Rick knows Mary?"

"Mary, our housekeeper?" Ryker's eyebrows shot up to his hairline.

"Yes. It was Rick that suggested she come here." Jenny's smirk didn't reach her eyes.

Ryker walked over and stood in front of Rick, dwarfing him. "Bennett, if you brought trouble to my family, you won't make it to jail."

"Mary was here, looking for Rick. When I told her Rick was shot, she took off."

"Jen, I get that you're angry with me. But enough already," Rick said, talking to her over his shoulder.

"Enough? Rick, I've finally had enough. I can't keep doing this with you or for you. Why was Mary here, and why did she take off?"

"She probably figured out who shot me," Rick muttered.

"Who shot you?" Ryker asked. "And what does Mary have to do with you?"

"It was Cole Slater, wasn't it?" Jenny asked. "He shot you. He was the one who abducted me, right?"

"I don't know. I'm sorry, Jen, but I didn't even know about you being abducted." Rick twisted around to see Jenny.

Ryker bent over and grabbed Rick by his jacket and lifted him off the couch. "We're leaving. Now." He stood him up and pulled his handcuffs out. "Richard Bennett, you have the right to remain silent—"

Rick reared back and headbutted Ryker. Ryker stumbled two steps and let go of his hold on him.

"Rick!" Jenny shouted.

Cold air blew into the room again when the front door's cold hinges squeaked. Adam brushed past Jenny, and reached over the couch and snatched Rick backwards, sending him tumbling to the floor. He reached down, grabbed Rick by his jacket, hoisted him up, and turned him around, pinning him against the back of the couch.

"Why do you insist on growing your list of charges?" Ryker said as he came up behind, yanked Rick's arms behind and ratcheted the cuffs on him. He finished reading him his Miranda rights.

Ryker walked Rick to the door. "Thanks for having my back."

"Thanks for the heads-up," Adam said to Ryker.

"Jenny, lock up behind me." Ryker opened the door and dragged Rick through it.

"I need to go too." Adam stepped around Jenny.

"Wait. Adam—"

"Jen, I can't. I can't do this now," Adam said as he walked to the door.

Jenny ran over to him and clung on to his arm. "Don't leave. You were right. I told Rick. I won't help him anymore. I promise."

"Maybe not this time. But what about the next time he comes around? What about if bail gets set? Are you going to bail him out?"

"No. You're right. I've been trying to fix everything for everyone. I've been doing what I think everyone needs. I'm sorry, Adam." Jenny tried to tug him back into the room.

"Jenny, I'm tired. I can't do this. I'm sorry, Boo." Adam slipped out of her grip and stepped through the door. "Lock up, like Ryker said."

Thirteen

Angela secured her dark hair in a bun at the nape of her neck and grabbed the badge off the sweater hanging on the chair, pinning it backward to the scrubs she'd taken from the locker room. She had shoved an extra set of scrubs in an unattended cart that she was now pushing down the hallway. She pushed past the officer in front of Rick's room and stopped, then backed up.

"I can't believe I almost went past Mr. Bennett's room," she said with a timid look at the officer. The cart's wheels squealed when she turned it around. "The police officer standing outside his door should have tipped me off." She gave the officer a small smile. "It's not like we have one of you guys here every day."

"Do you need help?" the officer asked.

"Oh, no, I got this, but I'm going to be in there for a while. You're welcome to take a quick break or grab a cup of coffee."

"Thank you, I'm fine." He gave her a quick nod, dismissing her.

"You sure?" She placed her hand on the door.

"Yes, thank you, ma'am."

"Okay, when I'm done here, before I head off to my next patient, I'll grab you a cup of coffee if you'd like. I made it myself when I started my shift. And I promise not to miss you next time." She gave him a big, toothy smile.

"I can't ask you to do that." His lips twitched, cracking his stoic demeanor.

"Well, let me know if you change your mind." She lifted her hand to her mouth and stifled a yawn.

The officer yawned, too.

"I guess they are contagious," she giggled. "Are you sure you couldn't use a little break? I promise I won't leave the patient's room until you get back. It will do you good to grab a cup and stretch your legs."

"You sure?" The officer looked up and down the quiet hall.

"Yes, of course. You guys work hard. Go." She flicked her wrist, shooing him away.

"Thank you," he said as he leaned over and pushed the door open for her.

She bit her lip and watched him slip down the hallway. The door closed, and she spun toward Rick.

His face lit up like he'd just won the lottery. "Angela! What are you doing here?"

"Getting you out." She pulled keys from her pocket and tossed them to him.

"How did you find me?" he asked as he unlocked the handcuff that had him shackled to the bed rail.

"Did you think I was going to leave town without you?" Angela walked over to Rick and kissed him, hard. "I've missed you. Let's hurry." She started to disconnect the machines they had Rick hooked up to.

"How do you know how to do that?"

"Epilepsy, remember? I spent a lot of time in the hospital when I was a kid. You pick up a few things." She went back to the cart and pulled out the extra set of scrubs and tossed them to him. "Put these on." She walked over to the closet and grabbed his things and shoved them in a bag. "Hurry. I don't know how much time we have."

"Yes, ma'am," Rick said, wagging his eyebrows. "Now, about that kiss."

"Is my darling husband dead?" Angela asked as she put the bag on the chair by the door.

"Can you give me a hand?" Rick asked, fighting with the scrub top.

"How's the shoulder?" Angela walked over and inspected it as she helped him into the shirt.

"I'll live."

"Where's Cole?" She looked into endless baby blues that belonged to a man she trusted with her life. A man who made her heart beat wildly. A man who would do anything to keep her safe.

"Last I saw him, he was in my basement, bleeding."

"Did you shoot him?"

"We fought. I got his gun. I shot him and left him to bleed. From what I hear, he got out somehow."

Angela's hand came to her mouth. "I'm not free, am I?"

Rick tugged her over and pulled her into a tight hug. "Not yet, sweetheart. But you will be," he said as he placed a light kiss on her temple.

Angela pulled back and ran a hand down the side of Rick's face. "We can't be together without him gone. He will never leave me alone. You won't be safe, and I won't do that to you." She ran her hand down Rick's arm. "You've been wonderful to me, and I couldn't have done what I've done without you. You've given me the courage to fight. And I want to fight for us, too, but Cole won't stop."

"Hey, don't worry about Slater. We'll figure this out, together. I told you I'd see this to the end, and I meant it."

"But you don't understand; he thinks he owns me. Everything and everyone is a game to him. People are disposable. His motto is 'May the best man win,' and he means he's the best man. He always wins, Rick. He won't stop until we're both dead." Angela backed out of Rick's embrace.

"Not this time. I promised you," Rick said to Angela's retreating back.

She opened the door and stuck her head out, not a soul in sight, and the police officer hadn't returned. "We've gotta go. You ready?"

Rick grabbed the bag, her hand, and slipped out the door. "Do you have a car?"

"Of course."

"Let's head to my parents' place, and then we can go. We'll figure out our next move when we're someplace safe."

Jenny stomped the snow off her boots and slipped her key into the lock. The door opened on silent hinges. Nothing looked out of place. She stepped inside, then immediately turned and ran back out the door and covered her mouth and nose with her hand. Bile rose in her throat. Snow drifted down and cooled her heated cheeks. After a couple of deep fresh puffs of air, she wrapped her scarf around her mouth and nose until she ran out of scarf, and faced the door again.

The odor inched and squirmed through her scarf as she made her way down the basement stairs. An invisible wall stopped her in her tracks when she stepped off the last step. Her hand added an extra layer over her mouth and nose. "What happened down here?" she mumbled through her hand and scarf.

Her eyes watered as the odor assaulted her. Apprehension filled her steps as she walked over to where Rick's belongings should have been from the pictures Ryker had shown her. All that greeted her was blood. The room was absolutely wrecked.

Couch cushions were everywhere but on the couch. Something peeked out from under the couch. She pinched the edge between her forefinger and thumb, then tugged Rick's bloodstained shirt he had been wearing the night he'd showed up at her house. She released the shirt and watched it fall back to the floor.

Slowly, step by step, she worked her way around this same room they used to play in as children, trying to avoid the blood and debris. Broken pool sticks scattered around the room, and thick, dried blood covered the pool table.

Surrounded by puddles of blood on the carpet, a tear slid down her cheek. "How did you survive all this?" Jenny needed to call the hospital and check on Rick's condition.

She took everything in again, but this time, she tried to detach herself. "All this blood cannot be from one person."

A coppery taste coated her mouth, filled her lungs and smothered her. She took off and ran upstairs and bolted out the front door again. She tore her scarf off and inhaled fresh, clean air. The freezing air stung her lungs, but Jenny welcomed every ounce.

She went back inside, over to the basement, and pushed the door closed with her foot.

The living room looked like it should. Rick was not alone in the basement, and whoever was with him had stayed down there.

In Rick's room, she looked around, and it, too, was untouched. It was exactly like it was the last time she'd been to the house. "I have no idea what I'm looking for. Why did I think I could do something?"

Jenny headed back to the living room and stopped. She turned and went to her father's den. Since Rick had been there, maybe he read the will.

The door to her father's den was wide open, like the last time she was here. Everything was as it should be. But the gun cabinet caught her eye. She reached to open the door, but hesitated when she noticed the black soot on the handle. She peered in through the glass, and some of Dad's guns were missing. Rick's favorites too. She grabbed a tissue and pulled open the drawer. The magazines were gone. Jenny licked her lips and sucked them in. She inhaled through her nose, then blew the air out through her lips.

The windows rattled and rocked in their tracks. The storm was picking up. She walked over to the window and watched the water pound the shoreline. The storm twisted the choppy waves, and their little boat slammed against their dock in the wind. The wind howled, and the snow was mounting.

She wasn't sure how long she'd been standing there, but it was time to take care of the things she could control. Rick wasn't one of those things. Her heart broke for him, and she prayed he was okay, but she needed to find Adam and settle things. He needed the truth and deserved the truth. Whatever it took to get his forgiveness, she'd do it.

She turned from the window and reached for the desk chair to put it back, then stopped and looked around again. "Why is the chair out of place?" Her eyes went between the gun cabinet and the will. "Did he finally read the will?"

Jenny's throat thickened. "Does he know now?" She flipped open the cover with her finger. Two envelopes lay on top, one addressed to her and one to Adam. Both in Rick's handwriting. "The letters."

The chair's wheels glided across the floor as Jenny rolled it over and sat. She slipped her finger under the flap and tugged it open. Her hand trembled while she held it.

The words read like a goodbye letter. He was leaving her everything, and he hoped to one day explain. He wanted her to believe in him and that he wasn't the person she thought he was. One day, she would understand that he was better than that.

A trip down memory lane, and a chuckle escaped when Rick mentioned her arm getting stuck in the pool table when she tried to retrieve her ball and he had to take apart the table to free her. *It's amazing what it takes to get one free. Sometimes, the things that don't make sense are the very things that will one day turn out to be the very thing that frees us.*

Jenny shoved Rick's letter under the will's cover. "Rick, what are you doing?"

"That's what I'd like to know."

Jenny froze; she didn't even dare to breathe. Her eyes remained fixed on the desktop.

That voice . . . His voice!

Leaving the hospital, the car, the drive, and the needle—it all came rushing back.

She looked up and locked eyes with Cole Slater. "It was you."

With white teeth gleaming through his slick bad-boy grin, he said, "I'm touched, you remember."

"W-what did you do to my brother?" A cold sweat crawled down her back and wrapped around her like the wind blowing outside.

"I wouldn't worry about him right now." Slater stepped into the office. "But you are exactly the person I need and who's going to help me. Come on."

Jenny scooted the chair back until she ran into the window.

Cole lifted a gun and aimed it at her. "We're going for a little ride. This time you're driving."

Jenny's eyes locked on the gun; they were wide, like she was facing an oncoming train while tied to the tracks. Ripping her gaze away from his gun to the blood on Slater's shirt, she said, "You're bleeding."

"I hear you're good at fixing us bad boys up. Maybe we should have brought you on board instead."

Slater pulled keys out of his pocket and tossed them to her. "You're driving."

They clattered to the floor, and Jenny scrambled to pick them up. "These are the keys to my parents' Lexus."

"Rick said you were smart. Now, let's go. Nice and slow," he said as he backed out of the office.

"I should look at your wound first." She pointed a shaky finger at him.

"You can do that when we get to where we're going. And hand me your phone."

Fourteen

Tethered boats rocked in their slips. Saltwater mixed with the falling snow slapped Adam's boots as he trudged his way down the dock. Wind-whipped ocean water sprayed his face. He ducked his head and hiked up the collar on his leather jacket as he made his way to *Sweet Lady*. He jumped and landed on *Sweet Lady's* platform with a splash. With a quick tug on the cabin door, it opened. Adam stooped and went in.

A lump lodged in his throat. *Sweet Lady* was the first boat he'd ever taken out alone. It was his favorite. His dad's too. He ran his hand over the captain's chair and flattened the curled duct tape. The tape curled back in on itself. Adam tried again. The tape rebelled again.

Adam turned his attention to the steering wheel and sat in the captain's chair. The wheel was smooth under his touch from years of hard work. It had been too long since he'd gone out on a run with his dad and his brothers.

Did he make a mistake not going into the family's business like his brothers? Was he really making a difference being a cop? Maybe Dave was right. Maybe he did make a mistake. Maybe everything in his life had been a mistake.

Adam slumped in the chair and noticed the snow was getting heavier, like the weight on his shoulders. As he looked out the window and upward, visibility didn't reach much past the boat's ceiling. "Heaven is out there, right?" The small cabin closed in on him and he closed his eyes. He waited.

Nothing.

His dad had told him to pray, but he said to get down on your knees and pray. Water sloshed in under the cabin door. There was no way he was getting on his knees in there. God was going to have to meet him sitting right where he was.

He waited again. Still nothing.

"This is stupid. God doesn't care about me or my problems. Dad's wrong."

A pen tied to the log book sitting on the sideboard rolled back and forth with the sway of the boat. Adam picked up the pen and flipped it over and under his fingers like a baton.

Dave's words replayed on a loop in his mind. *"Adam had to be the big crime fighter, but he couldn't even protect his brother. Make a difference, he said. His own wife doesn't even want anything to do with him."*

Dave was right. Jenny had been begging for this divorce for over a year. How long was it going to take him to accept the truth? She didn't want him. And if he were half the detective he thought he was, Mike wouldn't be dead, and his drug dealer would have been caught a long time ago. Every time he had a lead, it dried up. The guy was always one step ahead of him.

The howling storm swallowed the sound of Adam unzipping his jacket. As the wind lashed at the cabin windows, Adam pulled the divorce papers from the inside pocket of his jacket and unfolded them. He flattened and smoothed them over his thigh and picked the pen back up. Flipping to the first page requiring his initials, "Maybe it's time for everyone to have a fresh start," he said with the click of the pen.

"Don't do it," a deep voice said from behind him.

Adam's eyes closed and took a deep, steadying breath. His shoulders remained tight even as he blew out the breath.

"You'll regret it."

"What do you want, Dave?" Adam focused again on the line that needed his initials.

"To stop you from making a mistake."

Adam took another breath, held it, and counted.

"I mean it. You'll regret it."

"Like you care." Adam blew out the exasperation he'd been living with for months. Something needed to change.

"More than you think."

"It's what she wants." Adam held the tip of the pen over the line for him to initial.

"No, it's not. I saw her at the hospital." Dave's voice softened as much as the storm would allow.

The tension in Adam's shoulders worked its way into his spine and crept into the base of his skull. "Dave, I can't do this today."

"I'm sorry. I mean it. I saw your vehicle and stopped to say I was sorry."

"Fine. You said it. You can go now." Adam watched the snow slide down the window and avoided eye contact with his brother.

"I overreacted, and you were the one in my line of sight. I needed to blame someone." Dave stepped farther into the cabin and leaned back against the doorjamb with his hands deep in his jacket pockets. "Are you really going to sign those?" he said, catching Adam's gaze in the window.

"I would finally make Jenny happy." Adam's stomach felt like a million barnacles had taken up residence. How did he not see this coming? What was he missing?

"That's not what you want, and you know it." Dave's words were slow and measured.

"Maybe I'll quit being a detective and come work with you."

Dave shook his head and pushed off the doorjamb. "You know you don't want to do that."

"You think I walked out on the family."

"I never should have said that. I never should have blamed you yesterday."

Adam swiveled the chair and faced his brother. "Did Dad send you?"

Dave groaned and took a half step closer to Adam so they were almost toe to toe. "Not really. Not that Dad didn't have something to say, but this isn't what Mikey would have wanted. We both know that."

Dave offered his hand to Adam.

Adam stared at it, then looked at his brother. "How do we do this?"

"Well, first you reach your hand to meet mine," Dave said as one side of his mouth inched upward.

"No, I mean, Mikey is gone, and soon Jenny will be, too."

"Adam, can we please put this behind us and forget about all the stupid things I said yesterday?"

Adam nodded and cleared his throat. When he stood, he took Dave's offered hand and pulled him into a hug.

The storm's fierce wind whipped up outside and wrapped around the boat, smothering the sound of their grief over the loss of their brother.

Adam took a step back and kept his head down. He wiped his tears with this thumb. The divorce papers got crushed. Smoothing them back out as best as he could, Adam tucked them back into his pocket.

"Adam, don't sign those. Jenny loves you. I don't know what's going on, but wait a little while longer. And don't quit your day job."

Adam looked around the lobster boat. "You really don't want me around, do you?"

Dave snickered. "Come on, let's get out of here before the storm keeps us from going anywhere. I'm cold."

"Getting soft in your old age?" Adam said as he secured *Sweet Lady's* door and followed his brother.

The men jumped to the dock and started for their vehicles. The wind nipped at their ears and they picked up their pace. Adam's phone rang, and he fumbled with it, freeing it from the front pocket of his jeans. "Taylor."

Dave turned and frowned at Adam.

"Rick's missing," Ryker said. "Drew and I are at the hospital now."

"Hold on. I can't hear." Adam cradled the phone next to his chest. He turned toward Dave. "It's Ryker. I have to take this."

"Come by Mom and Dad's later," Dave said.

"I'll see you there," Adam said, and they both slipped into their SUVs. Adam waved to Dave and cranked up the defroster.

"Rick is missing. You're kidding, right?"

"There's more."

"I'll be there in fifteen," Adam said to Ryker.

"No. You know the captain doesn't want you anywhere near this case."

"Wait, how did that happen? Wasn't a uniform standing outside his door?" Adam pulled away from the docks.

"Yes, but a nurse came by and assured him she'd keep an eye on Rick so he could get a cup of coffee."

Adam muttered to himself and no longer needed the heat on. "I'm going to kill him when I get my hands on him."

"You might have to stand in line. There's more."

"Of course there is. We're talking about Rick."

"The nurse's description fits Mary's."

"Mary who? Wait, Mary, your housekeeper, Mary?"

"That's the one. Drew is reviewing security footage now with Dak."

"I'll head to Jenny's and see if she'll tell me anything."

Icy roads and falling temperatures mixed with Jenny's fear turned the roads into something made for dog sleds and the Iditarod. Light from the Lexus's headlights reflected off the veil of falling snow. It mocked Jenny. The roads demanded all her focus, but she couldn't get Rick off her mind and why Slater was looking for him. What had Rick done now? What had he brought to their doorstep? All she wanted to do right now was to call Adam and beg him to come and get her. Her selfishness put her in this situation. If she had leaned on Adam instead of kicking him out, she wouldn't be here right now.

With a vise grip on the steering wheel, Jenny maneuvered the car to a crawl heading north on 295 toward Brunswick.

"You drive slower than my grandmother. I'm bleeding over here, and unless you'd like to join me, pick up the pace," Slater grunted.

"I'm going as fast as the roads will let me." Jenny's slick palms tightened around the steering wheel. They had yet to see another car on the road, but she prayed someone would see them. But then what? What would they know? That it's just another crazy driver out in a snow-and-ice storm?

"You grew up here. I'm sure you can drive faster than this." Slater settled himself back against the door with his gun clutched in his fist as he propped it on his knee.

She flicked a glance at his gun, then back to the road. "I'd like to live." Jenny eased down on the accelerator anyway, and the car began to fishtail. Her stomach flipped, and a cold sweat trailed between her shoulder blades.

"Did you shoot Rick?" Her words tripped over each other as they rushed out of her mouth.

"The answer might surprise you," Slater said with a wink.

"Nothing about you surprises me." Her eyes jumped back to the gun, and Slater's hand slipped under his open jacket, cradling his side. "You're still bleeding. How bad is it?"

"Your concern is touching. But don't worry, when we get to where we're going, you can play nurse." His devilish grin toyed with Jenny.

Jenny squeezed her eyes shut, and she swallowed the ice forming in her throat.

A horn honked!

Jenny's eyes flew open, and she slammed on the brakes, sending the car into a spin!

Adam clicked on a table lamp by the door. "Jen, you here?"

The nagging beep of the security alarm answered him. Glad she hadn't changed the code, and that she remembered to use it, he turned off the alarm.

The dark, cold house was a comfort to the emotional roller coaster he'd been on the last few days that left his heart shredded. But he needed to find Rick, and he was sure Jenny was the key. He flipped on more lights as he made his way through the house, looking for either of them.

When he got to the master bedroom, he stopped in the doorway and took in the room in front of him. Bloodstains on the carpet and mattress from Rick were a reminder of when he had been in their bedroom on Monday. "What don't you ruin, Rick?" Adam clenched his fist, and he settled a hand on his gun.

Stepping over the stains, he went to the closet and pulled down a blanket. With a snap of the blanket over the bed, he laid it on top and covered the bloodstains.

Faded drops of blood still made their way to the front of the house. Adam went in the opposite direction, toward their guest room. Jenny's pillows were scattered on the bed, and her mother's Bible lay open on it. So, this is where Jenny had been sleeping. Was it since they separated or since Rick had been here?

The rest of the room looked like it was waiting for company. Before leaving, Adam straightened the pillows and plumped them up next to the headboard. He sat on the edge of the bed and picked up the worn Bible Jenny treasured and kept on the nightstand. The Bible was opened to Romans 10. The passage looked freshly highlighted. *"9 that if you confess with your mouth Jesus as Lord, and believe in your heart that God raised Him from the dead, you will be saved; 10 for with the heart a person believes, resulting in righteousness, and with the mouth he confesses, resulting in salvation."*

The Bible fanned closed when he clasped his hands over the spine and rested his forehead on the cover. *If it were only that easy. I did that and look at my life.* Returning the Bible to the nightstand, Adam went back to the living room.

He sat on the edge of the couch and tugged his phone free from his pocket. It slipped from his hand and thudded on the carpet, landing under the coffee table. He reached for his phone and knocked the remote off the shelf under the table. As he replaced the remote, he looked around the room and a knot formed in his gut. Nothing in the house had changed. It was just like it was when he lived here. Why hadn't Jenny changed a thing? What was she waiting for?

The corner of the papers on the coffee table fluttered when the furnace kicked on before they settled with the change in the air, drawing Adam's attention. More papers from her uncle, her attorney. Adam scrubbed his face with his hands and pulled the divorce papers out of his jacket. He snatched the pen off the table and signed and initialed on every line and left them on top of the stack. Once Jenny signed, her uncle could file, and she'd get her wish.

He was done fighting. He didn't have it in him anymore. If this is what she wanted, then he'd give it to her. It didn't matter what he wanted, and he wasn't sure what that was anyway.

Pushing himself off the couch, Adam walked over to the mantel. The corners of his mouth turned down when he stared at their wedding picture over the fireplace. The photographer had captured their families perfectly. He didn't know how the photographer did it, but every person was larger than life. Mike was grinning down at Melissa. Dave had his arm draped over Rick. His parents beamed. And Jenny's parents, alive and well. They were all so happy. He was happy. Jenny was happy.

It wasn't long after that they were all at Jenny's parents' funeral in the very same church they had been married in.

Adam snorted.

Church ... God ... "This is Him caring?" Adam tilted his head back and looked at the ceiling. "I thought you were about bringing families together, not tearing them apart?"

Adam turned back to the picture. "I'll always love you, Boo," Adam said to their wedding picture, clearing his throat.

Retracing his steps through the house, he turned off the lights. Jenny's file from Boston that sat on the dining room table caught his eye as he walked past it. He walked over and picked up the badge, then reached for the file.

"I just signed papers saying I'm not her husband anymore. I don't have a right, but is this why I signed divorce papers?"

Adam picked up the file. If paper could sting and weigh a hundred pounds, it was this file. He opened it. The top page was instructions to the hospital's online human resources portal to apply for a job. "Done" scrolled in Jenny's writing and a date at the top.

Adam closed the file and shoved it across the table.

Jenny was moving. Leaving him for good.

Fifteen

The snow churned in the wind, blanketing Maine's coastline. Tiny strobe lights danced in the glow of light from the lanterns hanging next to the garage doors as Adam pulled up in front of Jenny's parents' house. The electric-blue MINI Cooper Jenny's parents gave her after graduating from the nursing program sat in the driveway, covered in an inch of freshly fallen snow. "Well, at least she'll be happy to hear I signed the divorce papers." He shoved open the SUV's door and slammed it shut.

Stomping through the snow and wind, Adam fought his way to the front door and knocked.

"Jen. It's me. I need to talk to you." He clasped his jacket collar closed and turned his back to the storm and knocked again.

He reached for the handle and the door fell open.

What is it going to take for her to keep the doors locked?

The stench from the basement permeated its way up the stairs and greeted Adam when he stepped inside. It stung harder than the wind that slammed outside. His gag reflex kicked in, and he retreated in a jog back to his SUV. Struggling against the wind, he slipped into his SUV and grabbed his Mentholatum out of the center console. He dabbed it under his nose, then shoved the container in his jacket pocket.

He knocked the snow off his boots and pushed through the front door again. "Jenny. You here?" The cold air nipped at him.

A floor lamp in the living room was on, and the hall lights were on. But the house was quiet, too quiet.

Adam unholstered his Walther 9mm and kept it low and snug at his side. The carpet muffled his steps as he walked over to the basement. The door hinges creaked as he pulled the door the rest of the way open. One slow, deliberate step after another, he descended the stairs. The closer he got to the basement, the more time he took. Bracing himself with the handrail, he stopped and applied more Mentholatum.

He waited ... He listened ... He didn't hear a thing. The basement was so dark that not even the shadows came out to play.

Still bracing himself with the rail, Adam stuck a hand out from the stairwell and around the wall. He flipped on the overhead light and waited again.

A quick look into the room, then he pulled back and waited. He looked again, and from where he stood, it was clear.

He tightened the grip on his gun and stepped into the room. It was like he was seeing it for the first time. A storm brewed in his stomach that was just as fierce as the one outside. "Why did you bring this trouble to your sister's doorstep, Rick?"

What if Jenny came down here? What must she be thinking? Where is she?

The basement had nothing new to tell him, and he needed to find Jenny. He took the stairs two at a time as he rushed back up and closed the door. He cleared the rest of the house—no Jenny and no Rick. When he checked the garage, he noticed the Lexus was gone. Did Jenny switch cars because of the weather? Did Rick take it? Were they together?

Everything else in the garage looked to be in place. Adam called Jenny again and was greeted with her voicemail.

He tugged the door in the kitchen closed, secured it, and turned the kitchen light off. The front door opened. Adam slipped into the shadows of the kitchen that offered him a bit of protection. He raised his weapon and listened.

"It's about time you got here," he said as walked into the living room and stowed his gun.

Ryker turned at the sound of Adam's voice. "Find Jenny?"

"No." Adam motioned for them to follow him and he led them to the den.

"Where's Jenny? I see her car's here," Drew asked.

"Not here. Her parents' car is gone, so either she took it or Rick did."

"But if Rick took it, where is she?"

"That's the question of the hour." Adam rubbed his tight neck. Exhaustion was settling into his bones. "I'm off the case, but this is still my family. I'll call in the missing Lexus and maybe we'll get lucky."

Ryker walked over to the windows and watched the storm beat against the shoreline. "We have a missing Rick, a missing Jenny, and a missing car. And Mary was seen on the hospital security feed."

Adam turned to Drew. "Did you ID her?"

He finished typing a text and put away his phone. "I did, but it wasn't very useful. We can only place her at the hospital, not with Rick."

Adam called the station and reported the missing car. He laid his phone on the desk and looked at Ryker. "Doubt they'll find the car. I hate to ask the obvious, but didn't you run a background check on Mary before you hired her?"

A deep growl escaped Ryker. "I wanted to."

"Amanda?"

Ryker nodded. "The most I could've done was run her plates."

Drew came to stand beside them. "I could have done it for you. Amanda never would have known."

Ryker looked Drew up and down. "Maybe I should keep a closer eye on you."

He chuckled. "Nothing like that, but I may have been able to find something you couldn't," he said with a non-committal shrug.

Adam turned to the desk and flicked the corner of the cover on the will. A piece of paper stirred when the cover moved. He tugged it free, pulling an envelope with it. The letter was addressed to Jenny and the envelope to him. "Did uniforms sweep this room?"

"They should have," Ryker replied. "Why?"

Adam waved the letters at Ryker. "I wonder how long these have been here?"

Drew walked over. "Maybe they left the desk alone. Nothing was disturbed when we were here earlier. The focus was the gun cabinet."

Adam pulled the chair over, opened his letter from Rick, and scanned it. Nothing that would help them until his eyes caught on the last paragraph.

Please, Adam, no matter what Jenny says, she needs you. You know Jenny is fiercely loyal, to a fault, even if that means giving up what she desperately wants, especially if she thinks it's best for someone else. Don't let her get away with it. Fight for her.

The last person in the world Adam wanted to be right was Rick, but he was. Rick was right. He couldn't give up on Jenny.

"Anything?" Ryker asked.

"Other than Rick is actually right for once?" Adam leaned forward, resting his forehead a little harder on the desk than he intended.

"That's a first. What about?"

"My marriage, of all things," he said to the letter. Adam straightened and flipped over the paper he was holding. "I messed up." Adam leaned back and his head thudded against the back of the chair. "I signed the divorce papers."

Ryker stood there with his hands fisted on his hips, then returned to the window. "Let's find Rick and Jenny and see where this leads. Then we can deal with that lapse in judgment."

Adam reached over and picked up the letter to Jenny and read it. He chucked both letters back on the desk.

"Nothing that will help us?" Ryker asked.

"Not really. He's giving the house to Jenny, then babbles about the time they were playing pool and Jenny got her arm stuck in the side pocket of the pool table. Rick had convinced her that her ball was stuck, and she had to retrieve it or she'd lose the game." Adam rolled his eyes.

"Let me guess, he had the ball the whole time."

Adam nodded. "He was playing her. But he said, '*It's amazing what it takes to get one free. Sometimes, the things that don't make sense are the very things that will one day turn out to be the very thing that frees us.*' I think it's in reference to the pool table. But why bring it up?"

Ryker's phone rang. "Detective Scott." He turned and looked at Adam. "How many? Anyone hurt?"

When the call ended, he slipped his phone back into this pocket. "Two cars were spotted in a ditch on 295. One matches the description of Jenny's parents' Lexus."

"Already? Was Rick in it? Jenny? Both of them?" Adam stood, and the chair smacked into the window.

"Don't know. Uniforms are tied up, but they'll get there as soon as they can."

"Who called it in?"

"A snowplow driver. He saw them in a ditch and requested help."

"Well, did he say who was in the car?"

"No. Apparently, he didn't stick around."

"So he left the scene of an accident. Jenny could be in that Lexus and hurt." Adam snatched his phone off the desk and headed for the door. Ryker grabbed his arm and pulled him back.

"What are you doing?" Adam yanked his arm out of Ryker's grip.

"You need to stay put. Someone will get out there as soon as they can. We don't even know if it's Jenny's parents' car or if anyone's in it. You know, if Rick was in it, he's long gone."

"What if Jenny's hurt?" Adam watched Ryker struggle.

"What if you're wasting time and Jenny shows up and you're not here?"

"I'll go," Drew said from behind them. "You stay here. Maybe Jenny or Rick will show up. I'll let you know what I find."

Ryker tossed Drew his keys. "Go."

Jenny reached up and felt the goose egg on her forehead. Her fingers came away sticky. She looked out the windshield and only saw black. How long had she been here? She looked around the interior of the car. Slater slumped forward on the passenger window. She bent down to get a better look at him. His eyes were closed, and his chest rose and fell.

She felt around the seat and under the seat. No gun. He hadn't moved.

She squinted at the darkness, but it was useless. She couldn't see a thing, and the last thing she wanted to do was wake the convict next to her.

Jenny looked outside again. It was dark. From the way the car tilted, they were in a ditch. She tugged on her handle and the door opened. Against the darkness, the dome light shone like the sun.

"Going somewhere?" Slater slurred.

She froze.

"You weren't going to leave me, were you, sweetheart?" Slater cradled his abdomen.

Jenny heaved the door shut. "It looks like we're in a ditch. I was going to try to figure out where we were."

"Nice driving. Didn't you grow up here?" Slater pushed himself up in the seat and rubbed his neck.

"You should really let me look at your wound. The bleeding isn't slowing."

Jenny watched Slater close his eyes. She wasn't sure if it was from pain or annoyance.

His grip loosened on his abdomen as his head slumped against the window again.

Jenny reached for the door handle again when the Lexus filled with light from an approaching vehicle. The vehicle drove past them, then stopped. She watched the snow on the windshield glow red as the vehicle backed up and got closer to them.

She glanced over at Slater. He hadn't moved.

A car door slammed. A shadow approached her car. Was someone going to help her? Was she going to get out of this? What if it was someone looking for her and Slater? What if it was the person they were on their way to see, and they came looking for them?

Jenny's heart raced up her throat and skidded to a stop.

A man walked to her side of the car and tapped on the window. The beam from a flashlight blinded her and lit the interior of the car. She shielded her eyes with her hand to block the light. The door opened, and she was pulled from the car.

"Jenny? Are you okay? Is Rick in there with you?"

Jenny squinted to see. "Drew?"

Slater moaned.

"Go! Get in the SUV," Drew said as he shoved her toward his vehicle.

Jenny scrambled and skated on the icy road as she made her way to Drew's vehicle. She fumbled with the door handle and finally tugged it free and scurried into the SUV. Her fingers were numb, her hands were shaking, and she couldn't feel her toes. She turned backward in the seat so she could watch Drew pull Slater from the car and arrest him.

Drew slammed the driver's side door closed and walked around to the other side of the car. He pulled out a gun that appeared to be too big to be department issued, opened the door, and leveled it at Slater.

And fired!

Sixteen

The SUV continued north on 295 at a speed above what Jenny was comfortable with. She hadn't stopped shaking since she had climbed into Drew's vehicle. Never did she think tonight was going to be like this. Her plan was to go to her parents' house and check things out. Instead, she was kidnapped, saw Slater shot, and still had no clue what really happened to Rick or what he was mixed up in.

"Did you have to shoot him? Did he wake up and try to shoot you?"

"It will be fine, Jenny. I just took care of a problem." Drew never took his eyes off the road.

Drew's nonchalant and casual tone didn't settle her nerves. It only made them worse as his words spun around in her head. Why didn't he call this in?

"Why aren't we heading back to my parents' house? Or to the station? Don't you need to call in what happened? Was there anyone in the other car?"

Drew didn't even look at Jenny. He slowed and turned off the highway, weaving his way up a long driveway, and then pulled up to a massive iron gate.

Jenny leaned forward and looked out the window. "Wait. I know this place. I was here for a hospital fundraiser last fall. This is Robert Harris's house."

Drew waved to the man in the security booth as the gates opened. "That's right. You missed the party my uncle threw me when I made detective. Robert Harris is not only on the board at the hospital you work at, but he's also my uncle."

Jenny's eyebrows crinkled. "Why are we here? Isn't he in Florida right now?"

"He just got back." Drew gave Jenny a charming smile that was a little too fake. "I just need to make a quick stop. It won't take long."

Drew continued up the driveway and circled around the snow-covered fountains. He parked and led Jenny to the massive double-doors.

The door opened before they arrived, and a man motioned for them to come in. "Your uncle is expecting you."

It wasn't much warmer inside than out. But maybe that was fear and not the temperature.

Jenny glanced around the foyer and strained to listen to the hushed conversation Drew and the man who opened the door were having. It was useless. She couldn't hear a thing.

Jenny shoved her hands deeper into her coat pockets. *I can't do this on my own anymore. I don't want to be scared and alone anymore.*

Adam walked out of the den and headed for the basement. He pulled his Mentholatum from his pocket and dabbed it under his nose again. Then passed it to Ryker. "You're going to want this."

"Why are we going downstairs?" Ryker opened the jar.

"There has to be a reason Rick brought up the pool table. It's too random."

"And you want to check it out?"

"Don't you? We know he's been hiding out down here since he's been back. What do we have to lose? We're stuck here, waiting. And Rick's letter is digging under my skin."

Adam stopped at the bottom of the stairs until he could get his gag reflexes under control.

"Leave it to Rick to destroy his own home," Ryker said as he walked around the room.

Adam went to the pool table and ducked under it.

"What are you doing?" Ryker asked.

"I'd really like to not get my arm stuck if I don't have to." Adam stood up. "But it looks like I need to follow Jenny's lead."

"Did Jenny ever tell you which pocket?"

"Nope." Adam started in the corner pocket and fished around in both directions. When he got to the fourth pocket, the opposite corner pocket, his fingers made contact with something. It clanged in the channel and slid out of his reach. He tried the pocket on the other side and stretched a little farther and grabbed it. He tugged himself free and pulled it out.

Ryker let out a low whistle. "I wonder what's on that little gem?"

A thumb drive lay in Adam's palm. "I don't know, but I intend to find out. If this is the reason for all of this," Adam said as he motioned around the room, "I can only imagine what's on this."

They jogged up the stairs and made their way back to the den, only to realize there wasn't a computer or laptop to be found.

"Who doesn't have a computer these days?" Ryker asked.

"Jenny's parents. I know they liked to leave that kind of stuff at work, but I was hoping there would be something here." Adam looked around the den. "They used tablets or their phones at home." He tapped the thumb drive on this thigh. "As soon as Drew gets back, I'll run to Jenny's and use her computer."

"I can stay. Go now. If Rick shows up, I can handle him. I owe him one anyway." Ryker's voice turned lethal.

"Just one?" Adam deadpanned. "Call me if Jenny or Rick show up or if you hear from Drew."

"Will do."

Adam tucked the thumb drive into his front jeans' pocket and started down the hallway. Something snapped, then clicked in the kitchen. The sliding door bumped and thudded on its track. He slowed his steps as he saw Rick and Mary slip into the kitchen.

"Whose car is out front?" she asked Rick.

"The MINI is my sister's, and I think the other is Adam's. So we have to be quick."

"I don't like this," she hissed. "Why are we here, any-way? And if they're here, we shouldn't be. Can't it wait? Do we really need to be here?"

"I left something downstairs and I shouldn't have. I need to get it, and then we'll be safe."

"How can you say that? Slater is still out there some-where. We'll never be safe and I'll never be free," she cried.

"We'll take care of that problem before we leave town," Rick replied. "Stay here. You don't need to see the basement. I'll be right back."

"No. I'm going with you. What if your brother-in-law sees me? Or your sister?"

"Right. Promise me you won't look. We'll get in and out."

"Looking for this?" Adam stepped into their view and held up the USB drive between his thumb and forefinger. Rick took a step forward.

"I wouldn't go any further." Adam held up his gun in his other hand. "Even as angry as I am at you, I really don't want to shoot you. Now, let's sit down." Adam motioned to the dining room table with his gun.

Rick and Angela sat down beside each other.

"I thought you were—" Ryker stopped in his tracks when he saw Rick and Angela sitting at the table. His hand went to his holstered gun.

"Save me the time of looking at this." Adam waved the USB drive. "What's on it?"

"First, I want to know something," Ryker said and turned toward Angela. "You lied to me. And to my wife. And to my mother-in-law. We've been nothing but good to you. Amanda adores you. Why did you bring this trouble to us? And I know Mary isn't your real name. What is it?"

"Angela. I-I-I'm sorry," Angela said. "I needed to hide. I needed a safe place. I had to get away from my husband."

"And my home was it?"

"It's my fault," Rick interjected, clasping his hands so tight the muscles in his forearms tensed, and a vein popped to the surface. "I told her about Otter Bay, and I suggested she look for work with Amanda. Jenny had told me she was pregnant and might need some help."

"But what you did was bring trouble to our town." Adam tightened the grip on his gun.

"Trouble was already here. Didn't your brother just die because of it?" Rick pointed out.

"You're mixed up in it, too, and now you're trying to drag Jenny into it!" Adam's voice rose.

"No, I'm not. I'm trying to protect her!" Rick shouted.

Angela reached over and touched Rick's arm to calm him down.

"Because of your actions!" Adam's pulse roared in his ears.

"That was never my intention."

"It never is. What's on the drive, Rick?"

"Information."

"What kind of information? Stop playing games!" Adam took a step closer.

"Information that will bring down Robert Harris's crime operation."

Adam felt like he had just been slapped. "Robert Harris. Robert Harris, that supports the hospital? The same hospital Jenny works for?"

"Wait, Robert Harris is Drew's uncle," Ryker said.

"Why haven't we heard anything from him?" Adam slid his gaze to Ryker, then turned his attention back to Rick.

"You better start talking." Adam walked over into Rick's space and grabbed the back of the chair. "If anything happens to my wife, your sister, you're not going to have to worry about Slater coming after you." Adam tipped the chair back until the front legs rose off the ground and pinned him against the wall.

Jenny pulled her coat tighter and hugged herself. She still didn't know what they were doing here. Why hadn't Adam come for her? Why did he send Drew? If Drew knew she was in trouble, Adam must have known. Why didn't he come? Where was he? *I know he's upset with me, and he has every right to be, but if he had come, I could have explained everything to him and told him not to sign the divorce papers.*

"Drew, I'm so glad you could make it," Robert said as he extended a hand to Drew and walked into the foyer.

"You know Jenny Taylor, I believe," Drew said as he motioned to her.

"Yes, of course, it's a pleasure." Robert's smile didn't reach his eyes. He looked older than Jenny remembered, and his hair was thinning. Drew towered over him.

Robert turned his attention back to Drew. "Did you take care of the problem?"

"I did."

Slater was a problem for Robert Harris? Jenny tucked her hands in her coat pocket again and realized she never got her cell phone from her parents' car.

Robert turned his attention to the man who opened the door. "Mr. Dayton, please escort Mrs. Taylor to the kitchen. She looks like she could use a warm-up. And please get her something for that nasty bump on her forehead."

"I'm fine, really." The tremble in Jenny's voice rivaled the chill that was running through her.

"I insist. Mr. Dayton will take good care of you," Robert said firmly.

Jenny took a deep breath and slowly let it out, but her words still came out shaky. "Drew, can I borrow your phone? I'd like to call Adam."

"Mr. Dayton will take care of you. Will you please show her to the kitchen?" Robert said as he directed Drew out of the foyer.

Can this night get any worse?

"If you don't start talking, Ryker will take you both in and I'll drive. I'm sick of this, Rick!" Any louder and Adam's voice would have rattled the dishes in the china cabinet. Rick's chair thudded to the floor when Adam shoved off the chair. He stood over him with his arms crossed. Blood boiled and the veins on his neck bulged.

"I got mixed up with some bad people," Rick mumbled and looked away.

Adam twisted his body toward Ryker. "Do you have your cuffs?"

Ryker reached into his back pocket and tossed them to him.

Adam grabbed Rick by his jacket collar, jerked him out of the chair, and spun him around, pinning him to the wall. He had him cuffed before he could fight back.

"Stop! You're going to hurt him. He can't bleed again!" Angela shouted.

Adam turned him around and shoved him back in the chair. "Now. Let's try this again. Because next, I'll drop you in my car, and we'll be on our way to the station." Adam gave Angela a look that dared her to move. "Both of you."

"Start at the beginning," Ryker said.

"I didn't want Jenny to have to take care of me."

"Stop right there. This has nothing to do with Jenny. This is all on you, Rick. You made your choices, bad choices. And it started long before your parents' car accident."

Rick looked away. "I was trying to make my way. Robert said he could use help and would love to work with me. Before I knew it, I was in too deep and involved in his drug trafficking. He's using the hospital to funnel his drugs through Otter Bay and the entire East Coast. A few people in the hospital help him."

"How did you meet him?" Adam asked.

"It doesn't matter."

"It does to me." Adam leaned on Rick's chair again and tipped it back. Rick jerked forward, trying to keep his balance.

"You don't want to know."

"I want to know," Adam ground out.

Rick gave a slight shake of his head and glanced at Angela. She gave him a slight nod.

"Mike. Your brother introduced us through his dealer."

"I don't believe you. Mike had his issues, but he wouldn't have been in this deep." Adam rammed the chair back against the wall again and let it smack to the floor.

"He had a habit to support and debt to work off. He did what he needed to, I guess," Rick said.

"No, I don't believe it." Every word came out in a growl. Adam paced.

"Why do you think they killed him? He was a loose end, a liability."

Ryker stepped between a pacing Adam and an ashen Rick.

"So none of this bothered you? What Robert was doing to our community or what danger he brought to your sister?"

"This isn't what I intended. But it's no different than the danger you bring to Jenny with what you do." Rick's voice goaded Adam.

Adam lurched around Ryker, grabbed Rick out of the chair, threw him against the wall again, pinning him with a hand on his chest and the other back in a fist, ready to strike.

Ryker grabbed him and pulled him away from Rick. "This won't find Jenny," Ryker said.

Adam stormed away, and Ryker pointed to the chair.

Rick sank into the seat.

Angela gasped through her hands.

"Why haven't we heard from Drew?" Adam stopped pacing. He looked between Ryker and Rick.

Rick started to stand.

"Sit!" Ryker hollered at Rick and pointed to the chair again.

"You should also know that Harris is Robert's professional name for the hospital. His legal name, and the one he operates under is Hargrave."

Ryker took the chair across from Rick and Angela. "So it's Drew's uncle who's responsible for bringing drugs into our community. Do you know how many drug arrests we've made? Do you know how many overdoses there've been in the last year alone?"

"Is Drew mixed up in this?" Adam interjected. "Is this how it's gone unnoticed for so long?"

"I don't like this," Ryker said, shaking his head.

"What do we really know about him?" Adam asked.

"His parents moved to Florida a couple of years ago, but he stayed. He said he didn't have much family but an uncle through marriage who wasn't here that often and Drew saw him even less." Ryker watched Adam pace.

"We need to find out more."

"His record is spotless. I'd trust him with my life, with my family," Ryker said.

"But what if we're wrong?" Adam asked. "We don't know that much about him. We need to find out more."

A text message pinged Adam's phone. He ignored it.

"You might want to check that," Rick said.

"I have a few more questions for you first." Adam rubbed his chin as he was trying to put the pieces together.

"He's right. What if it's Jenny?" Ryker said.

Adam pulled his phone from his pocket and swiped it open. "It's Drew."

"What's it say?" Ryker stood and looked over Adam's shoulder. Adam punched the message open.

Found Jenny. No Slater. No Rick. At my uncle's. Please come.

"Why is he asking me to go to his uncle's place?" Adam looked over at Ryker, then at Rick. His phone pinged again.

Rick show up?

Adam debated what to tell him. He knew Jenny's life was in danger. His chest constricted like a screw being overtightened. The muscles in his neck and shoulders pinched, like someone had a wrench in his back.

No.

Drew replied: **Let Ryker wait for Rick.**

Adam waited for his phone to ping again. "This is wrong."

Be there as soon as the weather allows. Jenny okay? he replied.

Adam's phone went off again with Robert Harris's address. "We know this is a trap," Adam said through a clenched jaw. "And they have Jenny. If anything happens to her, I'll kill you myself, Rick."

"This is all my fault. I never should have come," Angela said through tears. "I'm so, so sorry."

"Yours and Rick's," Ryker said. "But you are right, this smells like a trap," he said to Adam.

Rick cleared his throat. "It's a trap. They want you two separated. You'll be easier to dispose of."

"Give me your phone," Ryker said to Rick.

"I don't have one. I lost mine, remember?" Rick replied.

"I do," Angela said with a hiccup.

"Untraceable?"

That got a dry chuckle out of her. "Of course."

Ryker turned to Rick. "Don't go anywhere. Got it?"

Seventeen

"Hand them over." Ryker held his hand out to Rick.

"Are you sure this is going to work?" Rick rubbed his wrists, then pulled the car keys out of his pocket and laid them in Ryker's hand.

"Has anything you've done since your return worked?" Ryker's tone made Rick take a step back.

Adam holstered his Walther as he came back into the dining room.

"Look, I know I screwed up. I'm sorry—" Rick looked between Adam and Ryker.

"I think it's too late for that. It's time for the grown-ups to fix this. And if your sister dies, I will be your worst nightmare." Adam walked over to the junk drawer in the kitchen and started rummaging through it.

"You don't understand," Angela piped up. "Rick has been trying to stop this. To stop Slater and get me out before Slater could kill me." She came around the table to Rick. "He never meant for any of this to happen. He didn't know Cole had followed him. And Cole was after me. You have to understand; Cole isn't like anyone you've dealt with before."

"And you brought that danger to Ryker and his family. And Rick may have gotten his sister killed." Adam scowled at Angela. "This is how you fix things?"

"What I don't understand," Ryker said, "is why didn't you go to the police or get in touch with Adam, Rick? You know we would have helped you."

"I thought this was better. I was going to handle Slater once and for all and disappear for good."

"And what about Jenny? After everything she's done for you, you were going to leave her? She loves you. Don't you understand? You were going to leave without even a look back?" Adam paused his search and waited for Rick to answer.

"Why didn't you say something at the beginning when you realized what was going on?" Ryker asked.

"I thought I could handle it." Rick tucked Angela in next to him.

"How'd that work out for you? Instead, you let all this danger come to our home," Adam said over the ruckus he was making in the drawer.

"Robert Harris brought all this to Otter Bay," Rick asserted.

"You knew what was going on, and you didn't say a thing," Adam challenged.

"I'm going to meet up with the captain. We'll be in position before you get there." Ryker checked the magazine in his gun.

"You can't do that." Angela cried. "Robert's men will see you. Cole said the security he has in place there is unlike anything he'd ever seen before."

Adam looked at Angela. "Who installed it?"

"I have no idea, but he said he has a nephew who's wicked smart with computers."

"Now you know why I used your phone to call the captain," Ryker said.

Adam slammed the drawer and pocketed Jenny's spare keys to her MINI.

"Hey, what happened to the Yukon?" Rick asked.

"Jenny loaned it to someone at the hospital," Adam replied, taking one last look around the kitchen. "I don't know the details. You can ask Jenny . . . if you didn't get her killed."

The hair on the back of Rick's neck pricked as he walked into the living room. He watched the lights of Adam's SUV disappear in the falling snow through the bay window. The scrubs Angela pilfered for them did nothing to fight the chill in the air.

Rick's room was untouched, and he found much warmer clothes to change into. Even a pair of old boots. He grabbed a hoodie for Angela, but before going back to the kitchen, he went to his dad's den.

He laid the hoodie on the couch and went to the gun cabinet. First, he looked to see what magazines were still there. Only the ones he'd taken earlier were missing. He tucked a .38 Beretta into his waistband. If the police took the guns he'd stashed in the garage, he'd need something. He lifted the Ruger 9mm and loaded the magazine, then laid it on the hoodie.

Rick stood in the den and fought the lump in his throat. Now was not the time to be emotional.

He walked over to the file cabinet in the far corner and found it locked. He had no idea where the key was for it so he grabbed the letter opener left on the desk and popped the lock. "Sorry, Dad."

The file hangers scraped on the rail when Rick pushed them back and forth, checking to see if they laid flat. They did. He brought them forward on the slides with the same result. Flat.

Next drawer . . .

A smile tugged at the corner of his mouth. "The gun and hoodie are for you." He loved her scent; he loved her. And he needed to free her of the monster that had her trapped.

"So, we're just supposed to stay here and do what?" Angela slipped Rick's hoodie on and rolled up the sleeves, then wrapped her arms around herself as she watched Rick rummage through his father's den. "What are you looking for?"

"I'm not sure. I'll know when I find it."

The file cabinet didn't give him anything he could use.

"Are we close to anything within walking distance here?"

"Not in this weather."

"Is there a computer here?"

"No. My parents were old-fashioned and left technology at work. At most, they had an iPad and their phones."

"Too bad. Maybe we could have found where Slater was staying while we waited."

"Wouldn't he stay with Robert?"

Angela sat on the arm of the couch. "Maybe. He didn't really like the guy."

"Did he like anyone?"

"Adam took the spare keys to your sister's car. There are no other vehicles here. What are we going to do?"

Rick froze. He slammed the drawer closed and walked over to Angela and kissed her. "You're brilliant." He tore out of the office and ran through the house to the garage.

"What are you doing?" Angela asked on his heels.

Rick was flinging cabinets open, rummaging through boxes, mumbling, "Please be here, please be here."

"What are you looking for?"

He reached his hand in a box and yanked out a pile of tubing.

"What is that?"

"How I'm going to end all of this."

Angela looked at him like he'd grown another head. "With tubing? Isn't that for a fish tank?"

Rick pointed to his old dirt bike. "I'm going to siphon some gas from Jenny's car and take the bike."

"I'm going with you." Angela's eyes brightened.

"No, you're not."

"You can't leave me here."

"You're staying. This ends tonight."

"You can't do this alone."

"You heard Ryker. The cavalry's been called in. I won't be alone."

"No, they'll arrest you. Slater will kill you."

"Not if I get to him first." Rick reached out and pulled Angela into his arms and held her. "You will be free of him tonight, Angela. I promise."

Snow and sleet pelted Adam's SUV as he navigated his way to Robert Harris's place. He flexed his fingers off the steering wheel, trying to loosen the death grip he had on the thing.

As he drove past the turnoff to where his parents' lobster business was, his dad's words replayed in his mind. *"Are you praying?"*

Why would he? God didn't listen to him. His wife was divorcing him and his brother was dead. Jenny's parents lived by their faith and they died in a horrific car accident. He didn't matter to God.

But he knew someone who did matter to God, and he knew he prayed. Adam hit the speed dial for his father.

"Son—"

"Dad, I need you to pray."

"Of course, but I told you, you can pray too. God will listen."

"Now is not the time for a lecture. Jenny's in trouble, and I'm on the way to get her out of this mess Rick created. Ryker too. We need your prayers. I'm sure Amanda would like her husband back in one piece."

"What's going on?"

"I'll explain later, but please keep us in your prayers tonight. We—I—need this to end, now."

"Whatever I can do, Son. Your mother and I will be praying. Please let us know what happens and if we can do anything."

"I will, Dad." Adam disconnected the call. The snow was beginning to lighten, but the roads were still slick. He added more pressure to the accelerator, and the wheels spun underneath him. He eased up a bit. All he knew was that he had to get to Jenny. Ryker's plan had to work, because there was no plan B.

Maybe there was. Maybe he could pray, but it'd never worked before. But who else could help?

He kept his eyes on the road and watched the snow tumble and float in his headlights. His dad wanted him to pray too . . . *Dad said God wants me to pray, that He can handle anything I throw his way, that he'll always listen. Then maybe it is time He got a piece of my mind, because from where I'm sitting, it looks like my life is some cosmic joyride for Him.*

"God . . . are you listening? Somehow I doubt it, but I'm going to try . . . for my dad. And others who tell me You listen. But you see, I don't think You do. At least not to me. You! You, God, are letting Jenny walk away from me! Out of nowhere, she decides that it's over. You hear me? Over! I thought marriage was important to You? Isn't it supposed to be a symbol of Your covenant with us? Or is it disposable, like us? No matter what I do, it fails. What is the point of it all?"

A tear rolled down his cheek as he continued to pour out his heart to God.

He was just beginning.

Eighteen

Spotless white granite countertop gleamed at Jenny as she wrapped her hands around a steaming mug of tea, letting its heat seep into her bones.

Goose bumps still ran up her arm, sending a shiver through her. Someone was watching her.

She looked over her shoulder at the door Mr. Dayton had exited, then around the room. White—everything was white. White walls, white countertop, white cabinets, and a travertine floor . . . white. Everything was white. Sterile. Cold. The hospital had more warmth than this place.

The barstool wobbled when Jenny hopped off. She hugged herself and rubbed her arms to chase the chill away as she walked around the room and inspected every inch of wall and counter space. There wasn't a phone to be found. And no cameras were in sight. But she knew if Mr. Dayton left her alone, she was being watched.

Everything from the way Drew was acting to Robert Harris's cold, impersonal reaction to her told her she was missing something. She had no idea Robert was Drew's uncle. But it didn't matter, did it?

She sat back on the barstool and propped her chin on her hand. "Why are we still here? Why is Drew even here? I can't sit here much longer. I need to find Adam. Maybe if I root through a drawer or two, whoever is watching me will come and stop me. Maybe they'll kick me out and send me on my way. And maybe I'll wake up and find out that my life has been nothing but a bad dream."

Jenny stood and shook the pins and needles out of her hands. "Why not?" The drawer closest to her effortlessly pulled open. There wasn't anything helpful in it. Drawer after drawer had the same result. The cabinets didn't have anything that could help either, and the last cabinet door banged closed.

The porch light shone through the French doors that led to the backyard, and it caught her eye. The snow was lighter now. She walked over and wondered if she'd set off an alarm if she went outside. She looked around the doorframe and didn't see any sensors, then laughed at herself: 007 she was not.

She leaned against the doorjamb and watched the snowflakes lazily drift down. She had to get to Adam and tell him how wrong she'd been. If she could go back and not have kept her MS from him, everything she'd done and been through, he should have been with her or at least had the chance to make the choice himself.

The only way she knew how to handle the life she was living was to control it. She was always there to care for others, and got into nursing to help others, but not to dictate their lives. Her dream was working next to her father. And it happened, but it wasn't long enough. "I miss you, Daddy."

It was ironic she now had a disease that no one could control, and one filled with unknown possibilities. So what did she do? Up the game and push away those who mattered most to her while trying to control them.

I'm done, God. I can't do this anymore. Please help me fix this mess.

Jenny wiped her tears and watched as the snow turned to flurries. "Ugh, what am I thinking? God, please don't help me. I haven't done a very good job at anything. Tell me what to do. Show me. Do it for me. I don't care, just don't let me take control anymore."

There was a lot she needed to undo, a lot of people who deserved answers and forgiveness she needed to seek. But it was going to be okay. Inhaling deeply through her nose and slowly blowing it out, she stood a little taller. "It is going to be okay."

Adam took a step back from the hulking man in front of him and stood a little taller. One look at this guy and he knew Jenny was in trouble. He fought to keep his tone even. "Where's Jenny?"

"I've got this. You can go," Drew said to Dayton as he walked into the foyer.

Dayton hesitated, never taking his eyes off Adam.

"I believe you're needed elsewhere," Drew said to Dayton, dismissing him.

"Did you bring it?" Drew asked Adam.

"Bring what?" Adam folded his arms over his chest and widened his stance. It was taking every ounce of control he had not to charge past Drew and search the house for Jenny. Then Robert Harris.

"You wouldn't be here if you didn't have leverage. Where's the thumb drive?"

"I don't have it. Your goon would have found it when he searched me and took my guns." Adam nodded in the direction Dayton had just gone.

"Looks like you're not here for Jenny. So, why are you here?" Drew cocked his head and raised a condescending eyebrow. He stood between Adam and the main house.

Adam wasn't leaving without his wife, no matter what. "You summoned me, remember?" Adam flexed his fingers, never breaking the mission-focused stare Drew fixed on him.

"I do. Look, I don't want any trouble, but I want Rick's thumb drive."

"No one knows where he is, remember? Maybe he's on the way here. I heard he has a few things to settle with your uncle."

"He's not worried." Drew continued to stare him down.

"I don't understand. All this time. You knew. You knew what happened to Jenny, and you knew why."

"I helped. I could tell you that Slater was one and the same the night he abducted Jenny and came back to the hospital."

"But I don't understand why you did it. Why a cop? Why work yourself like you did to make detective?" The worst kind of dirty in Adam's book was a dirty cop. It was an honor and privilege to wear a badge, to uphold the law.

"Don't worry. It wasn't hard. Besides, I like a challenge."

"So all along, you were dirty. This was all to protect your uncle. Your uncle, who just happens to be Robert Harris. How could you watch those we swore to protect die from the very thing your uncle was pushing?"

Jenny tightened the belt around her coat, and her hand bumped the door handle. She tried it, but it didn't budge. Not wanting to be cooped up like a caged animal, she said loud enough for any camera or microphone to pick up, "Well, let's just see who's watching me." Jenny headed for the kitchen door, and it swung open before she reached it. A yelp escaped from her and she jumped back. "Mr. Dayton, I was beginning to think you forgot about me."

"Never, Mrs. Taylor," Mr. Dayton said as he closed the door behind him.

"Excuse me, please," she said as she gestured with her hand for him to step aside.

He didn't move.

"I need to find Drew. I'd like to get home to my husband, if you don't mind." Jenny waited. "Could you at least tell me where I can find a phone to call my husband to come pick me up?"

"Why don't you drink your tea? I'm sure Mr. Harris will be back soon."

Heat crept into Jenny's cheeks, and she let out a frustrated grunt. She turned toward the counter. Then turned back and opened her mouth to speak.

"Life has a funny way of working out. I never intended to work for my uncle, but as time went on, I saw the family business as a legacy."

"Family business? Legacy? I thought your parents moved to Florida?"

"They did." Drew's words were guarded and filled with warning.

"And they're involved?" Adam pushed.

"I told you, it's a family business." Drew's eyes hardened and cut through Adam. "Jenny really has thrown you off your game. I hope it's worth it."

"Where is she?" Adam took a step forward.

Drew didn't answer.

"Jenny!" Adam hollered. He took another step closer to Drew. "Get out of my way. I'm finding my wife and we're leaving!"

"Jenny!" she heard through the closed door. "Get out of my way. I'm finding my wife and we're leaving!"

She froze mid-step. Adam. That was Adam! A wide smile split her face, and she darted toward and around Mr. Dayton.

"Ada—"

Dayton was quicker and wrapped an arm around her waist and clamped a hand over her mouth.

The more she struggled, the tighter his grip got.

She tucked her knees to her chest, and Dayton stumbled forward. They were close to the counter where Jenny had been sitting earlier. She tried to reach the counter with her foot. All she caught was air. They weren't close enough.

His breath on her ear, her cheek, the side of her face made her gag. He eased his hold, and Jenny threw her body weight forward. Dayton stumbled and mumbled something she couldn't make out.

Now her feet could reach the counter, and she planted both of them on it and pushed off, sending them both backward.

While Dayton tried to catch his fall with one hand, Jenny twisted out of his grip. She tripped over his feet and went flying into the glass hutch on the adjacent wall. The glass shattered, and the dishes crashed to the floor.

Dayton lunged for her and trapped her in the hutch where the glass had been, pinning her against the broken shelves and dishes. Shards of glass tore into her coat and ripped into her skin.

Growing up with Rick taught Jenny a thing or two about wrestling with boys and how to play dirty if she needed to. She brought her leg up between his legs, fast and hard. She shoved him off of her, and he tumbled backward, falling into the same barstool she had been in.

Jenny ran out the kitchen door and into the main living room. Right into Adam. His arms flew around her, and she yelled, "Let go, let me go!" as she beat on his chest.

"Jenny, it's me. Stop. Look at me, sweetheart." Adam caught her arms mid-strike and held them to himself.

Jenny sucked in a huge gulp of air. "Adam! You came!" She yanked her arms free and flung them around his neck and kissed his cheek, his nose, his other cheek—every muscle in her body turned to mush.

Adam held her close. "Come on, let's get out of here."

"No one is going anywhere," Drew said from behind them.

Dayton crashed through the door and stopped.

Jenny peered over Adam's shoulder at the gun Drew had trained on them.

Adam's heart leaped when he wrapped his arms around Jenny. She was here, in his arms—safe! This is where she belonged and where she would stay. Forever, if it was up to him. And he was going to do whatever it took to get her out of here, even if it was the last thing he did.

"You're not leaving," Drew said.

"Mrs. Taylor, I see you found your husband." Contempt dripped off every word Robert Harris said as he walked into the room.

"Please let us go," Jenny pleaded from Adam's protective hold.

Robert walked over to Jenny and reached out for her. Adam jerked her behind him. There was nothing friendly in Robert's expression. It was wild and controlled, at the same time, and he only had eyes for Jenny. Adam took a step back and tightened his protective hold on his wife.

"Drew, did Mr. Taylor give you the flash drive?" Robert asked, never breaking eye contact with Jenny.

"He says Rick still has it."

"He's lying," Robert said, tearing his gaze from Jenny. "Shoot her." Robert sneered as he walked away.

Shock crossed Drew's face for a split second, then he raised his gun and aimed.

"You're going to have to go through me." Adam's glare dared Drew.

"I can do it," Dayton said from behind them.

Adam's blood turned colder than it was out in the storm. When he looked over his shoulder, Dayton had a .357 Magnum aimed at Jenny. He felt Jenny shaking through his jacket as she pressed herself closer to him.

"Please, no. We have to find Rick. If you shoot us, he'll have no reason to stick around, no reason to give you what you want." Jenny's words quaked with her fear.

Drew was to the right of them, Dayton to the left, and Robert Harris right in front. Draw a few circles on the ground and you had a three-ring circus and Robert Harris was the ringmaster.

The living room window exploded and glass rained down. Drew collapsed; his gun skittered across the floor. He clutched his knee and rolled back into a fetal position, howling in pain!

Adam yanked Jenny to the floor and covered her.

Robert crouched behind the couch, inches from Drew's gun. He kicked the gun back to his nephew, then aimed his own at Adam.

"Are you okay, Jen?" Adam tugged Jenny into a seated position. He ran his hands up her arms, over her neck and face. "Tell me you're okay, please, Jen." Everything around him melted away. Jenny had his full attention. A bullet ripped past, sliced into the sleeve of his jacket, and threw him off-balance. Fire radiated up his arm, and he lost his hold on Jenny. Robert jumped, grabbed Jenny, and shouted, "Let's go!" to Dayton, leaving Drew behind on the floor.

"What about the drive?" Dayton asked.

Robert herded them toward the kitchen and away from the living room windows when the door swung open and Rick barreled through.

Robert yanked Jenny in front of him, snaked his arm around her neck, and pointed his gun at her temple. He stepped back and kept everyone in his sight.

Dayton turned his gun on Rick. "Give Mr. Harris the thumb drive."

Rick pulled out his gun and leveled it at Dayton. "Where's Slater?"

Drew groaned. "Gone."

"He's dead?" Rick asked.

"Yes."

Rick jerked his chin at Dayton. "You killed him?"

"I did," Drew replied.

Jenny gasped.

"Give the drive to Mr. Dayton. I won't hesitate to kill your precious sister," Robert instructed.

Sweat trickled down Adam's neck as he stood. His elbow burned from the bullet graze. Slowly, he reached between his belt buckle and jeans and slipped the thumb drive out. No matter what he did with it, he knew it couldn't save Jenny. *Please God, help us!*

Dayton lifted his gun higher, aiming for Rick's chest.

Rick mirrored Dayton's stance and took aim.

"I want that drive," Robert said to Rick.

Rick's eyes never left Dayton. "I told you I don't have it."

Robert repositioned his gun on Jenny, pressing it into her temple. She whimpered. "I want the drive."

"If you want your drive, Adam has it," Rick said and jerked his head in Adam's direction. "But I have your shipment."

"Rick!" Jenny hollered.

"Well, well, well." A genuine smile cracked Robert's face. "Mr. Taylor, I believe I have something you want. And I want something you have."

"Don't do it," Rick said. "Remember what he did to Mike?"

Dayton lined up his shot. Rick did the same and pulled the trigger.

Shots fired!

Rick crashed to the floor. Dayton did too.

Robert spun at the sound. Jenny reared back and head-butted Robert. Blood gushed from his nose and he staggered backward. She took off and ran to Rick and slid next to him.

"Adam!" Drew shouted.

He turned and caught the gun Drew threw him.

Robert regained his footing and stood over Jenny. His gun pointed at the back of Jenny's head.

Adam dropped to his knee, faced Robert, and pulled the trigger. Robert clutched his side, fell to his knees then hit the floor.

In two long strides, Adam was next to him, picked up his gun and tucked it into the back of his jeans. He checked on Dayton. No pulse.

Jenny's eyes were as big as saucers.

Adam's legs turned to jelly. Jenny was safe. Something freed in his chest and he could breathe again.

"Is Rick okay?" he asked.

"I'm fine," Rick said as he sat up. "He missed me."

Glass crunched, and Ryker and half the police department stepped through the back door.

Jenny slid back from Rick and ran to Adam. She flew into his arms and hung on. With her hands cupping his face, she said, "I'm so sorry. Please don't leave me. Please let me explain." She pressed her forehead to his. "I love you. I never stopped."

Adam leaned in and kissed her, sweetly, then deeply. His heart exploded. He wrapped his arms around Jenny and lifted her off the floor. "Let's get out of here."

Ryker cleared his throat.

Jenny and Adam hung on to one another and turned around. Ryker had Rick in front of him in handcuffs.

"I'm sorry, Jenny. I have to take him in," Ryker said, stopping in front of Jenny.

"No, I understand. It's time my brother paid for his choices. I'm just sorry it happened at all."

"Jenny, I love you. I'm sorry I dragged you into this mess," Rick said.

"Me too," Adam said and pulled Jenny a little closer, a little tighter, and kissed the top of her head.

Nineteen

Jenny stepped away from the EMT that had attended to her injuries, practically skipping to Adam, and if it were possible, she'd dance on the clouds. Things were far from where they needed to be, but for the first time in a long while, she felt like things might be heading in the right direction.

"I'm really okay." Adam winced and glared at the EMT dressing his graze from the gunshot. "It's just a scratch."

Jenny stepped up into the ambulance and slipped in next to Adam. Nuzzling up to him on his good side, she rested a heavy head on his arm. The adrenalin she'd been running on was ebbing, and exhaustion started to work its way into every inch of her. As she relaxed, contentment settled in. She could stay right here forever. Adam's scent wrapped around her and gave her the hope she'd been looking for since she was first diagnosed.

She forced herself to sit back up. "Let them do their job. Would you rather go to the hospital?"

"Don't be a baby." Ryker leaned on the ambulance door, readjusting his backward ball cap.

"Nice shooting back there. How's Drew doing?"

"He'll live." Ryker looked back at the house. "To think he was mixed up in all of this. For what it's worth, I don't think he would have shot Jenny."

"He had a gun aimed at her. That's enough for me." Adam wrapped his hand around Jenny's.

"Can you give us a minute?" Captain Danvers said to the EMT.

After securing Adam's bandage, the EMT hopped out.

"How's the arm?" Danvers asked.

"Barely a scratch." Adam draped his good arm around his wife and tugged her close. "But I think I need more vacation time," he said as he kissed her cheek.

Ryker rolled his eyes. "You didn't take the last one."

"We'll see what we can do." Danvers grinned. "I thought you might want to know. When Rick was taken into custody, we took him to the hospital to get checked out. Harris is in surgery. And they also picked up Angela from your parents' house. She's being questioned."

"Where has she been staying?" Jenny asked.

"My house. But that door just closed." Ryker re-adjusted his hat, then he let out a humorless chuckle. "What would have happened if I had had Drew look into Angela and he turned up something on her? She'd probably be dead. I don't like what Rick did, but his plan may have saved her life."

"Captain Danvers, is Angela going to be arrested?" Jenny asked.

"We'll see what she tells and if Ryker presses charges."

"Right. Amanda would love that," Adam said.

"When she's done being questioned, she can stay at my parents' house. It's Rick's house, anyway. Please let her know she has a place to go home to."

"I will, Jenny," Captain Danvers said. "Speaking of your parents. The Lexus is part of our investigation."

Jenny's stomach twisted, and she fingered the bandage on her forehead. "I don't want it. If I never see that car again, it will be too soon. A man was shot in it. Even if that man was Cole Slater, I still don't care to see it ever again."

"When we're done with it, someone from the department will reach out to you. At that time, you can tell us what you'd like us to do with it."

"Call Rick. It's his too." Jenny wrinkled her nose. "I don't care what he does with it, and I don't need to know."

She played with her wedding set and smiled as they kept talking. The sooner they got done, the sooner they wrapped things up, she and Adam could go home.

"Did you hear me, Jen?" Adam nudged her.

"No, sorry, I'm a little tired."

"The captain would like us to stop at the station tomorrow and give our statements."

"That's fine. Hey, what was the shipment my brother was talking about?"

Danvers exhaled. "That might be your brother's saving grace. The thumb drive had all Robert Harris's dealings, associates, and anything else your brother could find to copy." He shook his head. "It was a fluke that he got it."

"As I was escorting Rick out, he said he stayed with Robert because he wanted to bring him down. Slater had it in for him, though. Rick said he didn't move fast enough, and they figured out he had the thumb drive. He wanted to help Mike. And he was trying to help clean up Otter Bay," Ryker said.

The weight of Jenny's heart reminded her that her brother was alone and had been trying to protect those he loved. "I wish he would have reached out to us." Jenny looked up into Adam's eyes. "Or at least called you for help."

"Me too, Jen, me too," Adam said. "Wait, the shipment. What was he talking about?"

"Before a uniform took Rick to the hospital, he told me he rerouted Robert Harris's latest incoming shipment. Originally, it was coming here, but he had to go to Boston," Ryker said.

"The captain there, my old partner, A.D., called me a few minutes ago and received the shipment. Rick not only rerouted it, but he tipped off the authorities," Danvers said.

Adam whistled. "Who knew Rick could do the right thing?"

Pride filled Jenny. Her brother was going to be okay. He had some things to atone for, but he was going to be okay.

Adam stood and pulled Jenny into his arms. "If there isn't anything else, I'd like to get my wife home. She's exhausted and so am I."

The hum of the tires on the interstate soothed Adam, and he relaxed a little more into his seat. Jenny watched out her window and gripped his hand. Her warm hand hung on to his and he vowed to never leave her again, no matter what she said. He knew they had a lot to talk about, but he was here to stay

"Adam, when you came to find me tonight, did you see the Lexus in the ditch?" Jenny kept her eyes on the road, scanning it for the car.

"No. I knew where you were. I was doing something else on my drive." Adam laced his fingers through Jenny's.

She adjusted her seat belt and shifted to face him. "What do you mean?"

The smile that tugged at his lips crinkled his eyes. "I prayed."

"You did?" Jenny's small voice filled with hope and maybe a little caution.

"And I called my dad, too." Adam nodded as he spoke.

"Really?" Her voice grew stronger.

"Yeah, but Jenny, I have a long way to go on this walk, and I'm nowhere near my dad or Ryker."

"I don't want you to be like them. I want you to be you. There's so much to learn. I have so many questions, Adam."

"Me too, Jen."

"Will you see Pastor Matthews with me?"

Adam stole a quick glance at Jenny. Her eyes were sparkling as she leaned closer to him.

"I'll do any marriage counseling you want." He could never say no to her.

"Marriage counseling? No, I mean for help—spiritual guidance. Adam, I see the faith my parents have and I want that too. I know it's there and I think you know it, too, because you wouldn't have prayed on your way here. And you wouldn't have asked your dad to pray if you didn't believe."

"I'm still working on that." Adam let out a pent-up breath and glanced over at Jenny. "Maybe we can do this together."

"I'd like that." Jenny's grin reached from ear to ear, and he wanted to make sure that grin was there every day.

"Adam." Jenny's voice had gone small and unsure again.

"What, Boo?"

"I am really sorry. I never should have shut you out. I thought I was protecting you, helping you."

"I know." Adam watched the reflectors sparkle in his headlights as they continued down the interstate.

Jenny fidgeted with the cuff of his jacket. "Adam, do you think you could come to my next appointment with me to see Dr. Laghari?"

"Does this mean you're going to tell me what's going on? Why have you been seeing him?"

"Can we wait until we get home?"

"No, I've waited long enough. Please, Jen, tell me now."

Jenny gripped Adam's hand with both of hers. "You know I love you, right?"

"Yes. Please Jen, don't drag this out."

Jenny hesitated and held her breath for a minute, then let it out. "I have MS, multiple sclerosis."

Adam's stomach bottomed out, and the road blurred for a moment. *How could she keep this to herself all this time? Oh, wow. And she didn't tell me. Why? Why was she afraid to tell me?* Questions rolled around Adam's mind at the same speed they traveled down the interstate. They mingled with each other, creating a confusing web of more questions. He had no idea where to begin or how to help or what to do. *How can I fix this?*

"Adam? Are you okay?" Jenny squeezed Adam's hand.

"Why did you think you couldn't tell me about it, Jen?"

Jenny swiped away the tear that snuck out. "At the time, I wanted you to have the life I'd never be able to give you. I didn't want your pity. I thought I could do it on my own."

"And now?" Adam reached over and turned down the heater.

"I still don't want you to give up your dreams for me, but I don't want to give you up, either. That may sound selfish and I'm sorry," she said as he reclaimed her hand.

"Jen, we are supposed to be making dreams together. We're in this together. I'm upset you're sick, of course, and if I could take it from you, I would, but truthfully, I'm a little hurt you didn't trust me."

"I do trust you and I know you'd run off and try to fight my battles—no matter what they are."

"So, you fight mine instead?"

"No."

"Yes." Adam cut her off. "You decided what my battles were or would be when you don't even know yourself."

"I'm sorry. I said I was sorry," Jenny sniffled.

"I know." Adam pulled into the driveway and left his vehicle idling. He unlatched his seat belt and turned to face Jenny. "But Jenny, you cannot keep this or anything at all from me. We're a team and have been since I was pulling your pigtails in the second grade."

"I know. I'm sorry. When I say I'm sorry, I mean it, Adam. I have so much to make up for. Please, Adam, can we start over?"

Adam picked up Jenny's hand and kissed each knuckle along the top. "I want nothing more than to be with you and to be with you every step of the way. Tell me, what do you know about your prognosis?"

"With everything going on, I haven't given it much attention, the attention it needs. But now, together, I can see what's next with you. Dr. Laghari has been helping tremendously, and without him, I'd be a bigger mess. So, will you go with me to my next appointment?"

"Jen, I'll go anywhere with you. I can't imagine being anywhere else. I love you, Boo."

"I love you, too, Adam."

"Oh, and Adam?"

"Yes, sweetheart?"

"You're not dropping me off, are you? You're staying, right? In our home tonight?"

"Oh, I'm staying. Tonight, tomorrow, and every other night . . . forever."

Epilogue

The permanent smile Adam wore had been plastered on his face for the last month. He glanced at the letter sitting next to him and his smile broadened.

Since everything went down, just a short time ago, God had already answered so many prayers. He still couldn't grasp the love God had for him. But He showed up time and time again. And Adam knew He would get them through whatever Jenny's MS threw at them.

His SUV dwarfed Jenny's MINI as he parked next to it in their driveway. It looked like his SUV could eat her car for a snack. He snatched the letter off the seat next to him and sprinted to the front door.

Above the handle, he ran his thumb over the nick from their dresser from when they'd moved in.

It meant home. Their home. He was home . . . with Jenny. And there was no better place he'd rather be than with the love of his life. He was in their marriage, for better or worse, in sickness and health. And with Jenny by his side, he was already the richest person alive.

Pushing the door open, he stepped into the house and squinted against the low lights. Candles flickered on the dining room table.

Words lodged in his throat. No matter how many times he tried to clear them, he couldn't.

He hung his coat up on the hook next to the door and walked toward the kitchen as he wiped the moisture out of the corners of his eyes.

A box wrapped in wedding paper lay on the breakfast bar between the living room and kitchen.

"Boo, what's this?" Adam said as he ran his hand over the box, letting the ribbon fall between his fingers. "Jenny, where did this come from?"

Adam picked up the box and shook it.

"No cheating."

Adam turned at the sound of her voice. He would never tire of seeing his beautiful wife. She looked happy, a genuine happiness he hadn't seen in her in a long time. And it looked good.

"Jenny, who sent this?"

"No one. It's for you," she said and leaned on the breakfast bar.

He drew his eyebrows together. "I don't understand. It's not our anniversary."

"It's from me. Open it." She covered her mouth with her hands, like she was trying to keep a secret from escaping.

Adam slowly started to remove the paper. A corner of his mouth ticked up. He knew that drove Jenny nuts, but he couldn't help himself. It was always worth the reaction and never got old.

"You're not going to get me this time. You need to open this," Jenny said, as her hands did a little excited clap.

Adam's heart raced, and wanting to know what was in the box overrode his desire to tease Jenny, so he gave in and tore off the paper. Slowly, he lifted the lid and pulled back the tissue paper. His eyebrows knitted even more, and he looked at Jenny. "Jen, what's this?"

She reached her hand in, and the pieces of paper tumbled through her fingers. With a twinkle in her eye, she said, "Look closer, Detective."

Pulling out the pieces of paper, Adam's face lit up with recognition. "The divorce papers. You shredded the divorce papers."

"That I did."

Adam leaned over and kissed Jenny's cheek, then her temple, then her nose. "I wondered where they ended up. I thought you had put them away somewhere."

"I love you, Adam. I never should have shut you out. I should have trusted you, trusted us."

Adam wrapped Jenny in his arms and inhaled her scent. "I love you, Boo. Nothing will ever keep me away from you."

Jenny cleared her throat. "I'm glad you feel that way. The hospital in Boston called again today. They've asked for a start date. Adam, I can't keep putting them off."

"I have a surprise, too." Adam reached into his back pocket and pulled out the letter, waving in the air before giving it to Jenny.

"What's this?" she asked as she unfolded the letter.

"Read it." Adam wiggled his eyebrows.

Jenny's eyes lit up as she read. "Oh, my gosh! You got the job! You're joining the Boston Police Department!"

Jenny flung herself into Adam's arms.

"That's right." Adam tightened his hold on her. "I gave my two-week notice today. I hope you don't mind?" he said, laughing.

"Are you kidding! I'm so excited to start our new life."

"Are you okay with not being close to Rick?"

"Rick needs to find his way. And I think he was already beginning to, but kept it to himself."

"So you think he and Angela will get married?"

"I hope so, but that's not my mountain to climb. He needs to sort this out for himself."

"I've never been happier, Mrs. Taylor."

"You say that now, but what if you don't end up with that big family and instead end up pushing me around in a wheelchair?"

"Then I'll be happy for us because I'll know that's God's plan. And I'll do my very best to rest in that." Adam took Jenny's face in his hands. "Jenny, I don't know what tomorrow holds for us, or even for me. But I know I want to take this journey with you. No matter where it leads us."

Adam's phone vibrated, and he pulled it from his pocket. Ryker. He silenced the phone.

"I promise, Jen. No regrets."

"I believe you." Jenny looked deep into Adam's eyes. "Adam?"

"Yes, Boo."

"I love you."

Adam captured her mouth with his.

His phone buzzed again. "I'm going to kill him."

"Maybe you should answer it."

"I'm off until Monday, and I plan to use every minute with my wife, planning our future. Maybe even take her on a boat ride to Boston. A little house hunting?" Adam nuzzled Jenny's neck.

His phone buzzed again.

Before he could silence it, Jenny hit the speakerphone button. "Ryker, it's Jenny. Adam is here and you're on speaker."

"It's about time you answered!" Ryker's tight, strained voice echoed through the phone.

"Is everything okay? Is Amanda okay?" Jenny asked and turned to the phone and picked it up.

"We just got to the hospital. She's in labor."

"We're on our way," Adam said, and disconnected the call.

"Rain check on Boston? Next weekend?" he asked.

Jenny took his hands in hers. "Are you sure you want to leave your best friend?"

"Honey, he's only going to be two hours away. And he's going to be pretty busy for eighteen or so years."

Jenny searched his eyes.

"Jen, there is nowhere I'd rather be. Our future is together, and it looks like God is sending us to Boston."

Jenny looked around their house. "I'm going to miss this place."

Adam blew out the candles on the table. Jenny turned off the oven and pulled out the casserole, and set it on the stovetop.

Adam grabbed their jackets and opened the door. "Are you ready to meet the newest Scott family member, Mrs. Taylor?"

Jenny slipped into her jacket. "Where you go, I go, Mr. Taylor." Then she slipped her hand in his as they walked out of their home . . . together.

"For this reason a man shall leave his father and his mother, and be joined to his wife; and they shall become one flesh."
Genesis 2:24

The Gospel

The gospel is the good news of what God has done in Jesus Christ. The good news is that those who profess Jesus Christ as their Lord and Savior will spend eternity with Him. (Romans 10:9-10)

God saves us through His Son, Jesus Christ. We are sinners, all of us, and we are separated from God because of our sin. We cannot fix this on our own. But God, by His power, provides the means of redemption for us in the death, burial, and resurrection of His Son, our Savior, Jesus Christ.

Salvation cannot be obtained by the efforts (or works) of man. It is only by the power of God, by His grace, through the gift of faith. (Ephesians 2:8-9)

When man fell (Genesis 3), it affected every part of man, of us - from our mind, our will, our emotions, our bodies, our spirituality—ALL of it! The fall corrupted all of God's creation. We are literally hostile toward God. (Romans 8:7)

God is holy and righteous, we are not. We are sinners and our sin condemns us to Hell, God's wrath, for all eternity. (Romans 3:23; Romans 6:23)

Thankfully, in the gospel, God, in His mercy, provides a way for us to come to Him. He sent a substitute for us, Jesus Christ. Jesus paid the penalty for our sin by His sacrifice on the cross - His death, burial, and resurrection. (1 Corinthians 15:1-4)

Our old nature died with Christ on that cross and was buried with Him. We are resurrected with Him to a new life. (Romans 6:4-8)

There is no other gospel. Anything and everything else is in vain.

So, what does all this mean? It means that we have hope. We have hope in the power of a living God to save us! (John 3:16)

The gospel of Jesus Christ will not only save you from the wrath of God (Hell), but you are given a new nature with a changed heart, mind, will, emotions, attitude, desire, etc.

(2 Corinthians 5:17)

This is the work of the Holy Spirit, to produce fruit in us by His power. Those who are saved by the power of God will always show the evidence of salvation by a changed life.

God calls everyone everywhere to repent and believe. Repent of your sin of unbelief and call on the Lord Jesus to be saved. Repent of your sins and seek His forgiveness. (Mark 1:15; 1 John 1:9)

Dear Reader

Thank you for reading Adam and Jenny's story! I love this sweet couple and I'm so happy I got to bring them to you. I hope you've enjoyed it as much as I have. It's only because of God's continued faithfulness that this story happened.

If you haven't read the Gospel, please turn back one page and read the Good News.

And if you haven't read Kane and Mia's story or Ryker and Amanda's story, please visit my website to learn more! And while you're there, sign up for my weekly devotional newsletter. As a newsletter subscriber, you'll also learn about the latest books and news.

May God bless you richly!
Jodi

JodiArtzberger.com

Also By

Otter Bay Series

Come Home with Me
Don't Give Up on Me
Don't Let Me Go

Devotional
Psalm 1, The Path of the Righteous

Visit my website for more information.